SKULLCRACK

SKULLCRACK

Ben Bo

LERNER
SPORTS
A DIVISION OF LERNER PUBLISHING GROUP

For my brothers Tim, Hugo and Chris.
And also for Alice, who has waited long enough.
And for Janie

This edition published in 2000 by Lerner Publications Company by
arrangement with Bloomsbury Publishing.

Text Copyright © 1998 by Ben Bo

First published in Great Britain in 1998
Bloomsbury Publishing Plc, 38 Soho Square, London W1V 5DF

Cover design by Zachary Marell

Library of Congress Cataloging-in-Publication Data
Bo, Ben.
  Skullcrack / Ben Bo.
    p. cm.
  Summary: Jonah, a troubled boy who escapes from his dreary life
with an alcoholic father by surfing on the coast of Ireland, discovers
that he has a twin sister with whom he has an unusual mental link.
  ISBN 0-8225-3308-1 (lib. bdg.: alk. paper)
  [1. Extrasensory perception—Fiction. 2. Twins—Fiction. 3.
Brothers and sisters—Fiction. 4. Alcoholism—Fiction. 5. Surfing—
Fiction. 6. Ireland—Fiction.] I. Title.

PZ7.B6293 Sk 2000
[Fic]—dc21   99-047395

Manufactured in the United States of America
1 2 3 4 5 6 – BP – 05 04 03 02 01 00

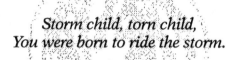

Storm child, torn child,
You were born to ride the storm.

Gallagher's field sloped gently away into the mist, dipped briefly into the scar of a path, then ended abruptly. Slashed. Sheer. Unfenced, except by nature.

Megan raced to the edge of the cliff and veered sharply away from the drop.

"Billy! Wait!" She was shouting now.

Her boots thumped into the trodden earth of the path. She was running again. Her legs aching. Her breath coming in painful gasps.

Ahead, her brother was moving fast, following the path as it snaked along the top of the cliff, dipping in and out of the mist that had snagged on the gorse and heather. Craxkull Point loomed before him, a smudge of dark rock stepping down into the fog.

"For pete's sake, Billy! You'll kill yourself!"

Megan sped up, staying as far away as possible from the ragged edge and trying to ignore the swift slither and rattle of the pebbles that fell away at her passing. She raced after her brother, breathless from the foot-thumping, heart-pounding run that had brought them up the lane from

Mulligan. White Bird Cottage had been deserted and the surge of hope she had felt when they got there died with the silence that had answered their shouts.

"He'll be down at Craxkull, I know he will," Billy had said.

Megan had looked up the lane, across the hedges to the misty greenness of Gallagher's field. The cliffs and the sea beyond had been completely hidden. "Then we'll need the boat," she had decided quickly.

Billy had shaken his head. "Will not."

Megan recognized her brother's furtive look. She knew it well and it made her suspicious. "What have you been up to, Billy Doherty?"

Billy hadn't admitted the amount of creeping and spying it had taken to find the hidden way down to the foot of Craxkull Point. He had become defensive. "I know stuff, that's all."

Megan resisted the urge to call him a sneak. "You'd better not be making things up again!" she said, breaking into a run once more.

Now, Billy had reached Craxkull Point and had stopped. He was breathing hard and standing dangerously close to the edge. He pointed into the mist as Megan ran up. "Told you! You told me to find him and I did. See?"

Megan swayed unsteadily as she looked down. "Where?"

She had expected to see the waves. She had expected to hear the surf. Instead, she saw only the swirling white and, in flat patches, the dark, unnatural calm of the sea.

"Jonah!" Her shout lifted a white bird out of the mist. It shrieked as it rose past them and turned away.

"There!" Billy said as a breath of wind cut through the milkiness.

At last, Megan saw Jonah. Far below. Standing at the water's edge, his surfboard lying at his feet. His head bowed.

"Looks like the psycho's praying or something," Billy said.

Megan silenced him with a jagged look. "Shut up for once in your life, Billy, and show me the way down! Now!"

She added, "Before it's too late," even though she knew it already was.

Jonah stood at the foot of the cliff where the path began and came to an end. He looked out into the mist. Beneath the eye-tricking swirls, the sea was heavy and dark. Flat. Dead.

"*Gaoth,*" he whispered. Then louder, "*Gaoth!*"

It seemed right to address something as ancient as the wind in Gaelic. "*Báisteach!*" He used the Irish name when he called to the rain, too.

He bowed his head and waited.

Nothing.

"*Stoirm!*"

A breath of wind stirred the mist, ruffling the brown spikes of his hair and caressing his cheek. The water moved, dark and glinting, as the wavelets lapped gently on the sand and caught the light.

"I know you're out there, so why won't you come?" He spoke directly to the storm. "I'll give you anything. Anything. Just bring the waves back to me."

The water drew back as if to contemplate the bargain, then rushed to embrace him, surging up around his bare feet in an icy froth that stole his breath. It gurgled softly and washed his feet, wrapping itself around his ankles before falling away again with a hiss that seemed absurdly loud for such tiny frothing bubbles.

Sighing, he waited. He was still waiting when the first of the big waves hit Craxkull Point.

Jonah heard them long before he saw them, at first mistaking the rumble for thunder. The brackish water surged beneath the mist. It swayed. Gulls erupted from the surface, sounding their alarm in a flap of wings as they came unstuck, rising half seen, half imagined, through the mist.

He sucked in a deep breath, recognizing a scent he could almost taste. Damp and rubbery. Salty. It was the scent of kelp that some hidden tide had dredged from the bottom and thrown up to perfume the air. Then, at last, they came.

He watched the waves rise up from the sea. Nurtured by the awesome forces of nature far out in the Atlantic and driven by winds not yet felt, they rolled toward him out of the mist. Walls of water more than nine feet tall. Curling at the lip as they stumbled on the hidden slab of the reef known as Skullcrack. Sparkling green and glorious before they fell with a bone-jarring crash on the black rocks of Craxkull Point.

"*Stoirm!*" Jonah laughed. He ripped off his sweatshirt and hurled it away, stripping off his land-skin until he was wearing only long board shorts.

Half-naked, he danced at the water's edge. His head filled with the new boom-crash beat of the surf. Arms thrown wide, laughing at the sudden sting of the spray on his bare skin, he turned in slow circles in the swirling mist.

"Jonah!"

It was like the distant cry of a gull but he heard it clearly even above the roar of the waves. He froze, one foot raised, arms outstretched, listening intently.

"Jonah!"

He spun around. "Who said that?"

The freshening breeze was opening holes in the mist and closing them just as quickly. The water's smoke twisted into wild shapes, seething with spinning vortices, tricking his eye and filling the fog with phantoms. One shape, however, seemed to remain constant.

He stared at it, straining for a better look until tiny lights started popping behind his eyes. Yes. He was sure of it now. The shadow had form, shape. There was a body. Arms. Legs. A head. And yet he could see through it. It was like an image projected on a movie screen, flickering and silent.

Jonah's heart threatened to thump its way right out of his chest as he recognized the shadow.

"Who are you?" he asked, his voice barely more than a whisper. "Why do you keep coming here?"

He took a step toward it, but the shadowy figure seemed frightened and moved swiftly away into the mist.

"Wait!" he called. "Please! Don't go yet! I won't hurt you."

A sudden gust tore through the mist and the shadow was gone.

"I saw her," Jonah muttered to himself. "I know I did this time."

He was kneeling, scooping away the sand with both hands. Digging like a dog, desperately searching for some clue that would make him believe himself.

A violent shiver shook his half-naked body and set his teeth chattering again, forcing him to clamp them shut.

"She was here. Right...here!" The words burst out of him as he slammed his fist onto a rock, mashing his knuckles into a bloody mess.

"Jonah!"

He heard the shout and looked up, heart racing at the sudden crunch of footsteps, the skittering click of the stones as they were caught by the toe of a boot and sent leap-frogging away.

"You are real!"

"Jonah!"

He recognized Megan and Billy, realized his mistake, and felt his disappointment deep in his stomach. He buried his face in his hands.

"Jonah!" Megan was breathing hard.

"Told you I could get down here," Billy said, sounding pleased with himself. He skidded to a halt, hands on hips, sucking and blowing through an O-shaped mouth.

"We were calling," Megan said, her words short and puffed. "Shouting all the way down the cliff."

Jonah turned his back on them, sitting with his legs tucked up to his chest, hugging his knees as he stared at the waves.

Billy tugged urgently at Megan's sleeve. He pointed quickly at Jonah's bleeding knuckles and hid his own hands behind his back as if afraid the same might happen to him.

Megan winced and knelt beside Jonah, her knees sinking into the pebbles.

"What have you been doing to yourself now, Jonah Ebbers?" she said with a sigh. She tucked her hair back behind her ear, only for the wind to free it again. Curling red tendrils flicked and danced around her face. She took his hand gently in hers.

Jonah watched as she wiped at the blood and wrapped her handkerchief around his knuckles. He looked into her eyes. They reminded him of the sea. Not blue, but green. Green like the deepest sea when the shadows of the clouds were on it. Flecked. Sad.

"Did you see her, Meg?" he asked quietly.

She frowned. "See who?"

"The girl."

Megan glanced at her brother. "Did you see anyone, Billy?"

Billy shifted uneasily then shook his head and started scuffing his feet.

Megan looked around. The mist was thinning fast as the wind got up. "There's no one here but us, Jonah."

"That's not true!"

She gave him that sad look. "We came all the way down from the top—we'd have seen someone going up."

"But I heard her calling my name."

"That was me, Jonah! Me!"

Jonah looked around, opened his mouth as if he were going to say something, then closed it without a word. He started to rock himself gently. Megan glanced at Billy and stood up. Jonah's hand flashed out and caught her by the wrist. He pulled her down beside him again.

"She was here, Meg. I swear," he said. "I saw her. I know I did this time."

"You're hurting me, Jonah," Megan said firmly.

Jonah stared at his hand as if it didn't belong to him, then realized what it was doing and forced it to let go. "Sorry."

She retreated a step or two to stand by Billy.

"I told you," Billy said in a loud whisper. He wound his finger in circles around his ear and nodded toward Jonah.

Megan hissed at him. "Stop that, Billy!"

Billy thrust his hands into his pockets, hunching his shoulders so that his head almost disappeared into the collar of his coat. "Everyone knows the lobsters are all barking in his pot," he muttered inside his coat. "Everyone 'cept my stupid sister, that is." His head popped up again. "He's just like his dad."

Jonah looked up sharply. "What did you say?"

Billy dodged behind his older sister.

"He didn't mean it, Jonah!" Megan said quickly.

Jonah was on his feet. "He's got no right talking about my father that way!"

Megan stood her ground. "Oh Jonah, you know what Billy's like," she said with a weak smile. "He doesn't think before he says things."

Being out of reach, however, had made Billy bolder. "If that's so, why don't you tell him why we've come? Go on Meg. Tell him."

Jonah looked from one to the other. "Tell me what?"

Megan stared at the ground.

"What is it? What's happened?"

"We've been looking all over for you," Megan started weakly. She paused as if searching for the right words, the kindest. "I'm sorry, Jonah. It's your father, he's—"

Billy couldn't wait to interrupt. "Down at the Crooked Finger again. Our dad saw him. Said he's acting like a wild man."

"Billy!" Megan stopped him.

"The Crooked Finger?" Jonah shook his head and glared at them. "No! He can't be. It's not true! Say it's not true!"

No one spoke.

Jonah turned away. "But he promised. He swore it."

"I'm sorry, Jonah," Megan said. "Truly I am."

Jonah scrambled to the top of the cliff and burst out through the brush, oblivious to the thorns that tore at his sweatshirt and shorts. He hit the path running, his surfboard under one arm, his shoes clutched in his other hand.

He didn't wait for the others. He just ran on, careless of the drop that dizzied away to the sea below. After winding his way along the cliff, he turned sharply across Gallagher's field. The grass was suddenly cool on his bare feet as he headed for the gate and the lane that lay beyond.

An old Land Rover was passing and he hurled himself at the gate, calling out to the driver. "Please! You have to help...."

Useless words.

He jumped down into the road, but could only watch as the Land Rover rattled on down the hill, turned the corner, and moved out of sight. He swore at the driver, pulled on his shoes and ran after the fading sound of the engine, shoelaces whipping the backs of his legs. He ran under the branches of the ancient oak that stood by Gallagher's farm. One bend, a short straight stretch, and he was standing at his front gate.

Beyond the patch that had once been a garden, White Bird Cottage was quiet. Empty. The windows were dark and cold beneath the low roof.

No smoke from the chimney. Only an empty space in the garage where his father's motorcycle should have been. Jonah dropped his surfboard by the back door and quickly set off down the hill into Mulligan.

The village began where the lane ended. The houses stepped down the hill on either side until they reached the harbor at the bottom. The fishing boats were in. He saw the Sligo Queen tied to the dock where the lobster pots were piled high. The harbor was deserted. The only sounds were coming from the pub.

The Crooked Finger tavern jutted out on the corner at the bottom of the hill overlooking the harbor. The sign creaked in the breeze, a painted finger beckoning, as if the old place wanted to share some dark secret that lay behind the leaded windows, glowing with a brownish, sickly light.

Jonah couldn't remember when his father had first taken him to that place. He seemed to have known The Crooked Finger all his life. "I won't be long." His father had always left him sitting on the step with that promise, and he had always broken it.

Jonah soon learned not to hope. After a while he hadn't even bothered to look up when the door opened and the sound of men's voices exploded into the night air. It had always been someone else leaving, someone else's father going home. Sometimes he had watched the men through the window, their red faces swimming in the ripples of the ancient glass, and had often wondered why his father always sat alone.

Then, one evening, Jonah had fallen asleep on the step and had dreamed he saw the pub change shape around him. The windows became slitted eyes. The door a sucking snout. Gradually it had changed into a monstrous pig. A hideous beast, slumped on the street, belching on a bellyful of black beer. Terrified, Jonah had run away and hidden among the lobster pots on the dock. It was there that old Fergus had found him.

At first, Jonah (who had been no more than seven or eight at the time) had found the skipper of the Sligo Queen almost as frightening as the pig-beast of his nightmares. The old man's face seemed cracked and cut with wrinkles. His wild hair, which sprouted from under his seaman's cap, was as gray as iron. However, the man's voice had been deep and calm, his words as smooth as weathered pebbles. Gradually, Jonah came to know him for what he was—a kind man.

After that night, whenever his father left him outside The Crooked Finger, Jonah would slip away and listen to the stories Fergus told. Sometimes the old man would tell them in the ancient tongue of Irish Gaelic, and his voice would fill with the rhythm of the sea. In time, Jonah learned to understand the Irish words without constantly asking, learning the language through stories without even realizing it. Fergus told of far-off places, of the great storms he called hurricanes, of giant squid and killer whales, of the sea and of the dolphins Fergus loved best.

"There's some around here," Fergus had once said, sucking on his pipe, "who'll swear salt that if the sea takes you, then you'll come back to life as a dolp'in."

Jonah had looked up from the lobster pots he was helping to stack on the dock. Fergus was staring out to sea, his pipe clamped in his teeth. Jonah followed the old man's watery gaze over the tight gray walls of the harbor, beyond the blunt colors of the fishing boats, past the three giant rock fingers of Gorag's Hurl, beyond Craxkull Point and out across the mouth of Killala Bay toward Downpatrick Head. West toward the Atlantic Ocean and then, America.

"Do you believe it, skip?" Jonah asked after a long pause.

Fergus removed his pipe and spat into the water lapping between the rusting hull of the Sligo Queen and the dock. "Maybe I do and maybe I don't," he said, clamping his pipe back between his teeth, "but one thing's for sure—them dolp'ins know more than any creature has a right to." The old man smiled. "So maybe it is true. Maybe they are the souls of the dead come back to life."

Since then, Jonah had always talked to the dolphins that often visited Craxkull Point. Out there in the surf he felt close to them, almost one of them, and he envied the freedom of the dead.

Thump! The door of The Crooked Finger opened and swung closed as someone came out. The sound brought Jonah up short. He looked up at the windows and spoke directly to the beast inside. "I won't let you take him, you know," he said. "No way! You're never going to win."

The pig-beast was silent. Brooding. Watchful.

The pub's warmth puffed into Jonah's face as he pushed open the door. It was airless and the tobacco smoke mingled with the smell of the beer and the faint odor of dried sweat. One of the men standing at the bar noticed him and nudged another. They all turned to look.

"Céard atá uait?" Big Bernard growled from behind his bar.

Jonah held the barkeeper's heavy gaze and answered his question in Gaelic. "I've come for my dad."

No answer.

Jonah looked from face to face. He knew them all by sight and name. All but one. A stranger was sitting by himself at a table in the corner. Thin-faced and pale, he had a round head that had been shaved bald, and a tattoo that curled across his cheek and up around his left eye. Jonah had noticed the stranger look up when he had opened the door, and he could feel the man's dark eyes on him now.

Big Bernard grunted suddenly. Jonah turned back to him.

"You'll find your dad out back, cooling off," Big Bernard said, jabbing a thumb over his shoulder. "And when he wakes up, you can tell Mr. Wexford Ebbers that his old mate Bernie would be most obliged if he would pay his bill. Cash will do nicely."

The men at the bar laughed.

Jonah could see the chalkboard nailed to the wall alongside a bottle of whiskey. A column of numbers had been chalked up. The numbers grew larger as they descended and ended with a total he knew they couldn't afford.

He wanted to shout at the men. He wanted to scream at them for allowing his father to drink. But he didn't. That would have shown them just how much it hurt. Instead, he just nodded and turned to leave the way he had come.

A movement caught his eye as he reached for the door. He noticed the stranger had his hands cupped, in the way someone might hold a small bird, and Jonah paused to look. The man opened his long fingers, spreading them wide. No bird flew out. Instead, an assortment of small bones dropped onto the table, knocking and rattling as they rolled among the rings of slopped beer.

Jonah watched as the stranger bent over them as if reading some coded message, picking through them with nimble fingers. The stranger smiled to himself and looked up.

Jonah backed away from those dark eyes, turned quickly, and was through the door in a moment. He slammed it shut behind him and leaned his back against the wood. He sucked in lungfuls of the cool autumn evening and blew out hard, trying to expel every trace of the stench that filled his nose and mouth. He could hear the men talking about him in the bar.

"There's madness in them Ebbers or I'm not a generous man," he heard Big Bernard say.

The men laughed.

Jonah swore a steady stream until he ran out of words bad enough to describe them.

Jonah found his father slumped among the garbage cans in the alley. He was drunk and snoring, still wearing his blue overalls from his shift at the cannery. His cheek was squashed into the rancid remains of a half-eaten fish dinner.

Jonah looked down at him as he lay in the gutter. "You promised me, Dad," he murmured. "You said you'd stop."

He was tempted to leave him where he lay—just let him sleep it off until morning—then he remembered the men in the bar.

"Let's not give them the pleasure, right Dad?" he said, scraping the mess from his father's face. He wiped his fingers before smoothing the hair from the sleeping man's eyes. The brown was flecked with gray, and his face was etched with deep lines. Jonah thought he looked very old.

The eyes flicked and opened, and a lopsided smile spread across his father's face as he recognized him.

"I just nipped in for a quick one, Jo," he said, the words slurring into each other.

"I can see that."

"It was the Finger's fault," his father said, blaming the sign over the pub door and grinning stupidly. "I swear it kept pointing at me."

"Come on, Dad. It's time to go home."

"You're a good lad, Jo," his father said, sitting up with some difficulty. "You never let your old man down." He tried to throw an arm around Jonah's neck, missed, and would have slumped back into the gutter had he not found a garbage can to hug instead.

Wex Ebbers was a big man, above average weight and height. The alcohol seemed to have dissolved his bones, turning him to rubber and making it hard to keep him steady on his feet.

"I can see two of you, Jo," his father said, squinting at Jonah from beneath drooping eyelids. "Two of you," he repeated, the stupid grin fading from his lips. He caught hold of Jonah's sweatshirt. "But there always were two of you, weren't there, Jo?"

"Whatever you say Dad."

Jonah had learned long ago to agree when his father was like that. He knew only too well how quickly the man's mood could change.

"But what's past is past, hey?" his father went on. "What's done is done, right?"

"Right."

His father looked at him under heavy eyelids. "Ah, what's the use?" he snarled. "What do you know anyway? Nothing, that's what! You're just a stupid kid!" He shoved Jonah away and decided he needed another drink.

Jonah knew better than to try to stop him. He watched as his father kicked away the garbage cans and teetered toward the back door of the pub. Staggering, hunched like a man twice his age, he took a step forward. Then two back. Suddenly his knees buckled and he nearly hit the ground again. Only then did Jonah dart in below the flailing arms and hold him up.

"You have to try and walk, Dad," Jonah said, gritting his teeth. "I can't carry you all the way home."

They stumbled out of the alley and into the street, his father leaning on his shoulder. The light from the street lights molded their shadows into one. Two heads, one body. A demon of monstrous proportions that danced around their feet as they staggered in and out of the light.

Then a voice came out of the darkness: "I see the sins of the father weigh heavy on the son."

Despite his burden, Jonah twisted like a cat. He saw a man standing in the darkness of a doorway nearby and recognized him immediately. It was the stranger from the bar. The Bone Man.

"*Cé hé tusa? Céard atá uait?*" Jonah blurted in Gaelic, then quickly in English too. "Who are you? What do you want?"

The Bone Man separated himself from the shadows. The darkness seemed to cling to him, pooling in the hollows of his cheeks and eyes, making a skull of his face.

Shivers started up and down Jonah's spine.

"They call me Jack," the Bone Man said with a slight bow. "And I couldn't help noticing you and your daddy there and thought you might like some help."

Jonah shook his head. "We're doing just fine."

"Is that so?" the Bone Man said, showing his yellow teeth as he smiled. "And I suppose you're going to carry your daddy all the way up that hill on your own?"

"I am," Jonah said, sounding more confident than he felt. He fumbled for a better hold on his father's belt and moved on quickly, keeping his eyes fixed on his feet. His heart beat wildly.

The Bone Man walked up behind him, his boots crunching the pebbles with an agonizing scrinching sound.

"You're quite right not to talk to strangers," he said, falling into step alongside Jonah. The stranger shifted the bladder-shaped leather bag onto his other shoulder and offered an arm. "But you shouldn't go worrying yourself. I know your daddy. We were drinking in the bar just now. He told me all about you, John."

"The name's Jonah," Jonah hissed, "and if you don't stop following us I'll shout until someone around here calls the cops!"

"No need for the police," the Bone Man said, holding up his big hands in a sign of surrender. "I'm not going to hurt you. I only want to help."

"Like I said," Jonah insisted, "we don't need anyone's help."

Jonah half-carried, half-dragged his father up the hill without stopping once, his tortured lungs pumping. All the while, he could hear the Bone Man following them. His footsteps measured and unhurried, as if he were stalking them.

When at last they reached the place where the houses ended and the lane began, Jonah was forced to rest.

Beyond the last of the street lights, the lane was lit only by a fitful moon. The three-quarter moon dipped in and out of the clouds, briefly lighting the road hedged with blackthorn along the top. It was a trap, and Jonah knew it.

"Wake up, Dad! Wake up!" he pleaded, shaking him roughly. "Someone's following us!"

His father stirred, opened his eyes, blinked, then came awake with a start. "What the—where am I?" he said as he staggered back, his arms flailing like a broken windmill.

Jonah tried to catch him before he fell, but it was hopeless. His father had thrown himself wildly off balance and he stumbled backward down the hill. The steepness of the slope didn't help. Although he waggled his arms desperately, his shuffling steps never quite caught up with the speed of his retreat. He tripped, let out a roar, and would have gone down heavily had the Bone Man not darted forward and caught hold of him.

"You leave my dad alone!" Jonah shouted.

He tried to pull his father away from the Bone Man but instead all three of them fell down. They thrashed about cursing until they disentangled themselves and sat up.

"All of which only goes to prove the proverb is right," the Bone Man said, fixing Jonah with a stony look. "Pride does go before destruction, and a haughty spirit before a fall."

"Look, I don't know who you are or what you're up to," Jonah said, "but I told you to leave us alone!"

"Well, that's a fine way to talk," the Bone Man said, "and me just having saved your daddy from a terrible accident."

"What do you mean saved? It wouldn't have happened if you hadn't been following us."

The argument would have gone on had not Jonah's father, who had been sitting on the road looking from one to the other in a daze, suddenly let out a yell loud enough to set most of the dogs in Mulligan barking. He declared his life well and truly saved and swore he would be in the Bone Man's debt for the rest of his life.

Jonah just groaned.

"It was nothing," the Bone Man said as he helped Jonah's father to his feet.

"Hey! Wait a minute!" Jonah said.

The Bone Man ignored him. "I'm a traveling man, you see," he said, throwing an arm around Wex Ebbers' shoulder.

"A traveling man—do you hear that, Jo?" His father sounded impressed. It seemed the night air had woken him up, but not cleared his head.

"Been all around the world," the Bone Man said, nodding. "Africa, India—you name it."

"India! Did you hear that, Jo?"

"I heard," Jonah muttered.

So it was that they went off into the darkness of the lane with the Bone Man telling them of his travels, sounding as if there wasn't a place he hadn't visited, or a tiger, lion, or crocodile—or any other reasonably ferocious creature for that matter— that hadn't tried to share his tent at one time or another.

Finally they reached the front gate of White Bird Cottage. And it was there, like the true professional he was, that the Bone Man began to close the deal.

"You wouldn't happen to know," he said, casually, "where a poor traveler like myself might find a bed around here? Just for a night or two, you understand."

That's all it took, just a few well-chosen words, for Jonah's father to start insisting the Bone Man could stay with them as long as he liked.

"He can sleep on the couch, Jo."

"But, Dad!"

"Well, that's settled then," the Bone Man said, and he was first through the door.

Jonah knelt to attach the leash to his ankle, pulled the zip of his wetsuit to the nape of his neck, and picked up his surfboard.

Two steps down the steeply shelving rocks took him up to his waist into the seething water. The cold bit through his wetsuit. He gasped and threw himself forward onto the flat of his board, ducking through a wave that reared up in front of him. The surge rolled over him. Breathlessly, he bobbed up on the other side and struck out for the froth and bubble that marked the break.

Behind him the cliffs climbed to meet the sky. The black rocks rose in jagged points and broken lines of strata, thrust up by the gargantuan forces that shaped the Earth millions of years ago.

On one side, closest to Mulligan, stood the three rock fingers that, legend had it, had been hurled into the sea by an angry giant called Gorag and had forever after been known as Gorag's Hurl. On the other, stretching out into Killala Bay, stood Craxkull Point.

Time and the forces of nature had scooped out the rocks between these two points to form a small bay. A bay that, to anyone who hadn't the trained eye of a surfer, might have looked like any other along that rugged coast. But the real secret of that place lay in what couldn't be seen.

As the cliffs had retreated, they had left their roots behind. Hidden. Buried beneath the water. Smoothed and flattened by the waves. A slab of granite stretched across the bay to form a reef that surprised and tripped the waves as they rolled in off the Atlantic, throwing up towering peaks of surf in lines that broke and peeled from Craxkull Point to Gorag's Hurl in a perfect left-hand break. This was Skullcrack.

Jonah ducked through the froth and freezing boil of the impact zone and came up gasping. Once he was out beyond the line where the waves were breaking, he sat up on his board. He caught his breath and rode the swell easily, straddling his board as it bucked like a pale thoroughbred tattooed with intricate curves and scimitar shapes. He studied the waves with a practiced eye. The surf was nine feet and clean. This was Skullcrack at its awesome best.

He counted the waves in each set. "Three, sometimes five." He spoke the numbers aloud, noting how nicely spaced and even they were.

A big set bumped up behind him. Jonah rode out the swell and trough of the first two, before deciding to take the third. With one easy move-ment, he pulled the nose of his board around to-ward the shore. Lying flat on his belly, he began paddling, thrashing the water on either side with his hands to pick up speed.

The wave, which had seemed ponderous from a distance, suddenly became supercharged as it reached Skullcrack. Tripping on the hidden reef, it rose until it towered over him, driven on by the momentum of the Atlantic storm that had given it life. Solid. Inexorable. Irresistible to the surfer who raced before it.

Jonah felt the familiar kick of the board as the surge caught him up, pushing him forward. He gripped the rails and made the jump, tucking himself up with one quick movement that brought his knees up to his chest. His feet slapped down on the flat of the board, he pushed up into a crouch, and suddenly he was standing, left foot forward—a natural.

He felt as if he had sprouted wings. He went swooping down the face into the trough of the wave, dipping low, then rising high to kiss the lip and feather a turn that plumed the crest with a white fan of spray, before dropping down the face once more.

He rode the currents until, inevitably, the wave began to close as it approached the shore and forced him off. And then, like Icarus on his doomed flight, Jonah's wings just melted away.

*

It had been a long night. The last Jonah had seen of his father, he had been sitting at the kitchen table with the Bone Man.

The two men had been taking turns sucking on a bottle of Old Agony, which his father had somehow managed to hide away for just such an occasion. The strong liquor had been having its usual effect on him.

"Who're you looking at!" his father had snarled. "It gets so a man can't even have a drink in his own house any more!"

Jonah had known then that his father wouldn't stop until the bottle was dry or he had drunk himself into oblivion. Worse still, Jonah had noticed the slanted looks the Bone Man kept giving his father. That Bone Man gave Jonah the creeps.

Jonah had taken the first opportunity he could to sneak away, creeping up the ladder to his bedroom where he had sat on the floor in the dark, his back square against the door. Fully clothed. Ready for trouble.

Midnight passed. The night stretched on. Gradually, the men's voices began to fade until silence had fallen over White Bird Cottage. It had been then that the demons had found Jonah.

*

The water slapped against the nose of his board as a wave billowed under him and brought him back to Skullcrack. He steadied himself, rode out the swell, and noticed the dolphins.

The dolphins were farther out. Swimming fast. Chasing a school of mackerel, they rainbowed out of the water every now and then as they skipped across the waves. He saw one break away from the rest of the school and turn toward the shore. As he watched the dolphin, the sunlight pierced the clouds, dropping fingers of light into the sea.

"My dad can't help it, you see," he told the dolphin softly. "It's the pig. It's got ahold of him. The others, they don't understand. None of them do, not even Meg."

Jonah had been up at first light, creeping out as his father slept. The night had turned the Bone

Man into a snoring lump under a blanket on the couch, and Jonah had been careful not to wake him as he climbed down the ladder, tiptoed across the living room and into the kitchen.

Breakfast had been a handful of crackers, slightly stale, and water straight from the tap, all swallowed with hardly a pause on his way out the back. He was already wearing his wetsuit, rubbered from his ankles to his waist, the top half hanging down like a half-shed skin. Outside, he stamped his feet into his shoes and picked up his board. By the time Megan and the others were catching the bus to school, he was catching waves off Craxkull Point.

The dolphin burst through the surface of bright water. For a moment it hung in the air, the pale gray of its belly exposed and glistening. Then it slipped back beneath the waves, vanishing as quickly as it had come.

"You cut school too!" Jonah laughed. He looked for the fin among the waves but couldn't find it.

He had decided long ago that school was no place for thinking. At least, not for thinking about important things. He knew of only one place he could do that. Out here, lost among the waves on Skullcrack.

Somehow the surf seemed to wash away the broken thoughts that constantly seemed to fill his head. The thunderous roar of the water drowned out the whispering voices of the demons that tormented him with his own self-doubt. Somehow, out here, things always seemed clearer. Better.

"But what if Billy's right?" He confided his worst fears to the invisible dolphin. "What if everyone's right about us Ebbers?"

He glanced instinctively toward the shore, half-expecting to see the shadowy figure of the girl standing at the foot of the cliff. His gaze took in the horseshoe of rock and climbed the line of the hidden path to the shrubs and red heather at the top. Nothing. No one. And yet....

He screwed his eyes shut and shook his head. "Why can't I just be like everyone else?" he groaned, "Normal!" He threw his head back and stared at the sky. "Is that so much to ask?"

He wrenched the nose of his surfboard around and charged with the next wave. He paddled back and caught the one after that. Furiously, he rode one after another until, gradually, the broken thoughts that had threatened to overwhelm him were washed out of his head. He tapped into the rhythm of the ocean. Merged with it. Became part of it. His soul was blending with something much bigger. Something without beginning or end. A glorious feeling of being.

A gull robbed him of it. Dipping to the water, the white bird settled briefly before exploding back into the air. Startled, Jonah looked up and instantly the fragile link with the ocean was severed. The rhythm lost.

"What did you have to go and do that for!" He shouted as the bird rode the wind effortlessly.

Suddenly, Jonah knew only great tiredness. He was numb to the bone with cold. Even the wetsuit that covered him in a layer of rubber could not keep it out. His feet and hands were blue. His hair had punked itself into spikes and his face was stinging with the salt.

But the waves were still pumping. In their thunderous roar, Jonah heard Skullcrack calling him. He tried to escape back into the waves, but now his body was stiff, his movements awkward. He chewed up the next wave badly, snapping a turn that was too tight. He caught an edge. The wave folded around him, closing on him in a seething froth and spilling him into the water in a blur of flailing arms and legs.

He came up just as the next wave in the set began to break. It curled over his head, hung for a moment, then dropped on him with its full weight. The maelstrom engulfed him, sucking him down to a place where all sounds were muted except the metallic swish and slap of the water. Then out of the violent swirl came the reef: Skullcrack!

The slab expanded to fill his vision. Massive. Cruel. Cracked and fissured, like the skin of some monstrous sea creature too long in its seabed.

Jonah slammed into it and was swept on by the current. The solid rush of water rolled him over and over without mercy, until—as if the monster had suddenly become aware of his presence— Skullcrack seemed to reach up with a gnarled claw and grab him by the ankle.

Pain shot up his right leg as the leash that attached him to his board went taut. Instantly, his forward rush ended. The current slammed him down on the rock again and again. Bubbles burst out of his mouth and nose in a silver cloud. Despite the mind-numbing violence, he knew immediately what had happened. His board was jammed in the rocks, holding him to the bottom.

Jonah fought back against the current, desperately trying to release the leash, tearing at his ankle with hooked fingers as the air in his lungs began to run out. Red-hot pokers were stabbing into his lungs. He was sure it was only a matter of time before his chest exploded.

His whole life seemed to squeeze itself into a single moment. It became concentrated, pure, as his mind focused on one thought—survival.

But every time his fingers found the Velcro straps around his ankle, the current surged and sent him spinning about helplessly. The creeping blackness threatened to overwhelm him, seeping in at the edges of his mind. Thick as pudding. Suffocating. Deadly.

He realized he was drowning.

When it came, the sudden jerk felt no more severe than any of the others he had endured. Jonah did not notice the leash go slack at first and only when the current suddenly swept him forward once more did he know he was free.

He caught a glimpse of something slicing through the darkness. Vaguely, he wondered what it was as it came spearing out of the gloom toward him. A moment later it slammed into his shoulder and face. Blood burst from his nose in a cloud of red, but he was beyond pain.

He fought with this new terror until he realized there was something familiar about its shape. He recognized it as his surfboard and hugged it to his chest. And as the last of his strength trickled out of him in a precious trail of shining silver bubbles, the board's buoyancy gradually began to lift him clear of the reef. Up out of the murk. Up through the weighted layers of water. Up toward the shimmering light and the life above.

*

Jonah paused as he reached the wooden gate leading out of Gallagher's field. He struggled to lift his board over it, then heaved himself after it, slithering down the other side.

He had never been so tired. His fatigue weighed on him like a lead suit, dragging his chin onto his chest and his arms down limply. It was all he could do to hold onto his board.

An age of time seemed to have passed since the waves had thrown him onto the rocks like a piece of driftwood. He had coughed up a stream of sea water and collapsed. Sometime later, he had opened his eyes and found a gull standing nearby, its wings tucked up neatly as it stood on one yellow stick-leg, watching him.

"I'm not dead yet!" he had croaked.

Jonah stumbled out into the lane and down to the old oak by Gallagher's farm. There he paused for breath, resting as he had many times during the tortuous climb up the cliff, until he was moved on by the sound of an engine and a horn blaring. He knew it was the school bus long before he saw it round the bend behind him.

He did not look back as the bus pulled in to make its scheduled stop under the oak where he had just been sitting. He heard the Gallagher sisters chattering as they got off and a hiss of compressed air as the doors closed. Faces peered down at him from the windows of the bus as it slid past and headed down the lane to Mulligan.

He didn't notice that Megan had gotten off until he heard her voice.

"Stop following me, Billy Doherty!"

"It's a free world. I can follow anyone I like," Billy answered back. Megan gave up on him and called out to Jonah.

Jonah didn't stop. She had to run to catch up.

"Jonah! Wait! Are you okay?"

"Why shouldn't I be?" He didn't look at her.

"Well, you weren't in school," she said. "And after last night. You know, your father...."

"He was drunk, yes! You can say it," Jonah hissed. "I found him in the gutter with his face covered in rotten fish. There! Now you know, so you can leave me alone."

"Rotten fish," Billy grimaced. 'That's gross!"

"Shut up, Billy!" Megan grabbed Jonah's arm, forcing him to stop.

"If you think that's why I've come—" she started angrily, but her breath caught in her throat when she saw his face. "Jonah! What's happened to you? You look terrible!"

"It was an accident." He turned away. "I was surfing. It happens."

"More like his dad's been beating him," Billy said, craning his neck for a better look. He whistled appreciatively at the darkening bruises. "No wonder he wasn't in school."

"That's not true!" Jonah snarled, scaring Billy across to the other side of the lane. But he could tell by the horrified look on Megan's face that the idea had taken root.

"Listen! My old man may not be perfect," he said, "but he'd never hit me. Not ever!" He shot a poisoned glance at Billy. "And I'll beat up anyone who says otherwise."

Billy drew a finger across his lips as if to show just how sealed they would be, then crossed his heart and hoped to die if he ever breathed a word to anyone of what Jonah's father had done.

'That's just what I mean—he hasn't done anything!" Jonah's snarl re-opened the split in his lip so blood trickled down onto his chin. He rubbed at it furiously and set off down the lane again.

"Mr. Morran was looking for you," Megan called after him. "I told him you were sick again, but I don't think he believed me." She fell in step alongside him and managed to drag her horrified gaze from his face just long enough to dig a book out of her school bag. "So you'd better read this. Mr. Morran is giving us a test first hour."

Suddenly all the weariness and confusion Jonah felt turned to anger. He snatched the book and shook it in her face. "What's the point of books or school or Mr. Morran's stupid history tests? It's all just a waste of time! There's no point in any of it for me!"

He hurled the book away in disgust. It flew through the air, fluttered briefly on white paper wings, then dropped dead into the mud and dung left by Gallagher's cows on their way to milking.

The wind riffled quickly through the pages.

Megan picked up the book. She tried to rub off some of the filth but only managed to smear it.

"I didn't ask you for it!" Jonah said, immediately regretting what he had done but unable to admit it. "I didn't want the stupid book."

"Oh yes, I forgot," Megan said, tight-lipped with anger. "Jonah Ebbers doesn't need anyone's help, does he? He just wants to be left alone so he can feel sorry for himself all the time."

"That's not true!"

"It is so!" Megan said, her eyes flashing. "Well, let me tell you, I do feel sorry for you, Jonah! I really do."

"What's that supposed to mean?"

"Sometimes, Jonah Ebbers, I can't help wondering if Billy might be right about something for the first time in his whole life."

Billy grinned, nodded, thought about what she had said for a moment, and then frowned. "Hey! What do you mean, first time?"

"Forget it, Billy," Megan said. "We're obviously wasting our time here. Let's go home."

Billy didn't want to leave, but Megan took him firmly by the arm and led him down the lane. They hadn't gone far before she looked back.

"Maybe everybody's right about you, Jonah," she said and added, "everyone except me."

With that she turned and dragged her brother away, with Billy grinning back over his shoulder at Jonah every step of the way.

Somewhere in the darkness, the demons of White Bird Cottage stirred. One by one, they cloaked themselves in shadows and, with pinched faces and unblinking eyes, came creeping from their lightless holes.

Jonah sat on the threadbare carpet with his back pressed against his bedroom door and listened. The whisperings, like the rustle of the branches of the cherry tree outside his window, or the murmuring of the wind in the chimney, or the restless scratch of the rats in the roof, didn't fool him.

He knew if he stared long enough into the darkness he would catch glimpses of them; some sitting cross-legged on the bookshelf, some dangling from the ceiling, others piled up on bent backs forming ragged pyramids in the corner by the closet. They were always quick to notice him watching, however, and would scuttle away. For a short while they would be silent. But, one by one, they came creeping back, to watch and whisper once more.

They were all whispering the same thing now, ceaselessly: "Billy's right. Everyone's right. Billy's right. Everyone's right."

Jonah pressed his fingers into his ears, but there was no escaping the demons. It was as if they were whispering right inside his head. Finally, when he could take it no longer, he decided to take his chances with the men below and escaped from his room into the passage.

An orange glow shone through the open trapdoor in the floor, deepening the shadows in the rafters above his head. He crept to the ladder that descended directly into the main room below and peered over the edge into the shadows.

The fire had settled in the grate, its dwindling light making shadowy lumps of the furniture: the couch, the chairs, and the old wooden chest by the window. To his right, he could just see that the front door was locked and bolted. To his left, over a gulf of shadows, the kitchen door was framed with thin cracks of light.

The ladder creaked as he placed his foot on a worn rung. He froze, alert. Stepped down. Hand after foot. Rung after rung. In silent count. Until one foot touched the floor, then another. "Dad?" he whispered.

A log settled in the fire, sending a shower of sparks up the chimney. The sudden flare set the shadows leaping and hopping, dancing on the walls and ceiling. For a moment, the living room seemed truly alive. But the fire settled again in the grate, the flames returning to a quiet flicker.

Jonah studied the light coming through the cracks around the kitchen door. He approached cautiously. The door wasn't latched and it moved slightly at his touch. A stripe of light fell across his face as he looked through the crack. Inside, he could see his father slumped over the kitchen table, one arm hanging down, the fingers curled up like a dead spider. An empty bottle lay on the floor where it had fallen. Jonah pushed the door farther and stood back, leaving it to swing inward. It bumped gently against the wall and he looked around. His father stirred in his sleep. There was no sign of the Bone Man.

"Maybe he's gone," Jonah murmured, hoping he was gone for good. He locked the back door quickly, sliding the bolts into place to be sure, before risking a quick look out of the window.

The moon hung low in the sky, one edge flattened as if it had bumped on the rim of the world and bounced. The moonlight turned the walls of the garden and the roof of the Swamp—the outside toilet—into silver, and transformed the half-buried skulls of the turnips rotting in the corner into zombies rising out of the earth in ranks. Jonah stepped back from the window quickly, cursing his imagination.

He was hungry but he didn't find much worth eating in the fridge, so he stepped back into the shadows of the living room. He felt along the wall for the light. Click. Nothing happened. Click-click, click-click. He gave up. Only then did he notice the Bone Man, standing in the shadows, watching him.

Jonah felt as if his guts had suddenly been sucked up into his stomach, iced and knotted. He backed away until he bumped up against the bookshelves, the jolt knocking the words off his tongue in a rush: "How long have you been standing there?"

" 'Deep into that darkness peering, long I stood there, wondering, fearing',￼" the Bone Man said, stepping forward so the firelight gilded his face. "Have you read much Edgar Allan Poe?"

Jonah shook his head quickly.

"Nevermore!" The Bone Man croaked the word and found something in it to smile about.

Meanwhile, Jonah's mind had raced through half a dozen reasons why the Bone Man might have been hiding in the dark watching him. Unfortunately, he hadn't been able to think of one that was good.

The Bone Man looked at the rows of books on the shelves. "Judging by all these, someone here must like reading. Perhaps it was your mother."

Jonah remained silent.

The Bone Man went on, "You can tell a lot about people from the books they read. What makes them laugh. What makes them cry. Books are like locked boxes." He glanced at the wooden chest by the window. "You never know what you might find when you open them up."

He turned his dark gaze back to Jonah. "Your mother died a long time ago, didn't she?"

"You've got no right talking about her!"

"Is that so? Well, then I'm sorry." A pause. The Bone Man sniffed the air, nodded as if whatever it was that he could smell proved something, then added, "It's like I thought, there's been much sadness here."

"Look, I don't know who you are," Jonah said, "or what you want from us, but I wish you'd go away and leave us alone."

"Want," the Bone Man said. "Everyone wants something nowadays, that's for sure." He sighed, sat down in front of the fire and poked the embers into life. He didn't look at Jonah when he spoke. "I don't suppose you'd believe me if I told you that I want nothing more than what you've already given me. A place to rest on my journey. A little food. Some company."

He shook his head and looked up at Jonah. "No, you think I'm a con man. You think I've come to sponge off of you. But you're wrong, young Jonah Ebbers, because I always pay my way in full."

"Who are you trying to kid? You haven't got any money!"

"Money? Who said anything about money? I possess something far more precious than that," the Bone Man said, reaching for his bag.

The zip rasped and the leather split open as if he had gutted it with a knife. Jonah watched with horrified fascination as the big hand went dipping deep into its guts, churning up the insides until it came out, clutching a small pouch. He loosened the string tying the neck of the bag and poured part of the contents into his hand.

"That's just a bag of bones," Jonah said.

The bones were different shapes and sizes, carved and worn smooth with constant fingering. Most were no bigger than the knuckle of his thumb and each was marked with a strange symbol that seemed to glow.

"These aren't just bones," the Bone Man said in a low voice. "They have great power."

"You can't fool me!"

"And you can't fool me either," the Bone Man said. "I knew it as soon as I saw you."

Jonah frowned. "Knew? Knew what?"

"That you needed my help, of course. That's why I followed you. That's why I stayed."

Jonah laughed. "So you're saying you're only here to help me!"

The Bone Man nodded.

"But you don't even know me!"

The Bone Man just smiled and turned back to the fire. He fed the flames with sticks, setting the shadows leaping and hopping again. It was as if he had the power to summon the demons of White Bird Cottage and make them dance.

Jonah edged toward the ladder.

"Have you ever wondered about the future, Jonah?" the Bone Man asked without looking up.

Jonah shrugged. "Sometimes."

The Bone Man reached into his bag and rummaged around until he found a small metal bowl and a silver box. He placed the bowl on the hearth in front of the fire, then he opened the box and took out a small cube no bigger than a sugarlump. He held it carefully between his thumb and forefinger and placed it into the bowl.

Jonah watched as he took a smoldering stick from the fire and blew gently on the glowing end. Its yellow brightness grew stronger. The Bone Man touched the tip into the bowl and the contents flared. The brightness faded to an ember. Smoke began to curl up from the bowl, drifting in the firelight as it trailed away in the shadows.

The smoke smelled sweet and sickly and caught in the back of Jonah's throat as he breathed. He coughed. "What is that stuff?"

"Incense. It will help to free your mind."

"Stinksense, more like!" Jonah hissed. "Put it out or I'll wake my dad!"

The Bone Man ignored the empty threat and closed his eyes. He breathed deeply.

Jonah glanced toward the kitchen. He could hear his father's labored breathing and knew he would be out for hours.

"To understand the future you must first understand the past," the Bone Man said. "Because it is the past that makes the present and shapes the future."

The smoke was making Jonah feel breathless and lightheaded. "Look, I don't know what you're doing," he said, "but I want you to stop."

"Don't be afraid. Clear your mind," the Bone Man said, closing his eyes. "Let the bones speak."

"No! It's stupid! I won't!" Jonah was beginning to feel dizzy. He couldn't think clearly.

"It is time," the Bone Man said as he opened his eyes.

Suddenly, those eyes were all Jonah could see. The Bone Man's face seemed to expand to fill the whole room. His dark eyes trapped the light so the fire seemed to be burning deep inside the man and not in the grate. Jonah could not escape them, no matter how he tried. Those eyes were everywhere, and all the while, the Bone Man kept dividing and then coming back together again. Jonah began to sway on his feet.

"Open your mind, Jonah," the Bone Man said, breathlessly. "Let me help you see."

Jonah shook his head. "No! Stay away from me! Just...leave...me...alone!"

He staggered to the front door, gasping for clean air, leaning heavily on the wall as his fingers fumbled with the bolts. First one, then the other slid back. Suddenly the door was open. He stumbled, slipped, and fell outside.

Jonah looked around, blinking in astonishment. Somehow, night had turned to day. Instead of the overgrown garden and the lane in the moonlight, he found himself standing near the top of a round hill.

It was a wild place, roofed by gray clouds. Unfamiliar. A place without trees or bushes where only coarse grasses dipped and bowed before the wind. Not far from where he stood, the side of the hill had crumbled away, spilling down the slope in a scar. Further off, beyond the hills that surrounded him, the sea shimmered in distant sunlight.

It started to rain. The squall blew up the side of the hill without warning, firing the rain drops at him like lead shot. They stung his face and hands, but as he turned to go back inside, he found that White Bird Cottage had vanished.

He spent wild moments searching until the bitter cold and sting of the rain drove him to look for shelter. He saw some rocks and made a dash for them.

The rocks were farther away than they looked, and the rain had almost stopped by the time

Jonah flattened his back against the nearest. He raked the drips from his hair and glanced nervously around.

The stones were huge, cold, gray, and silent. Giant pieces of granite standing at equal intervals around the top of the hill, they formed a perfect circle. Their points bluntly needled the clouds that hurried overhead.

He stepped away from the stone at his back and looked up at the strange marks and symbols carved in the flat of its face. Ancient designs were etched deep in the rock. Each stone was similarly carved but each symbol was different.

"This is weird," he said to himself. "Where am I?" He tried to remember how he had gotten there but he couldn't.

Jonah didn't notice the stone in the middle of the circle until he stumbled over it. It was round and flat and half hidden in the grass. He sprawled across it, landing hard on his knees and scraping the scabs from his knuckles so his right hand started bleeding again. As he sat up cursing and sucked at the tiny red beads on the back of his hand, he noticed the stone beneath him had begun to change.

Jonah jumped up and stared at it in amazement. In seconds it became transparent. Only the shape of it remained, flat and heavy in the grass, and yet, surprisingly, when he reached out tentatively and touched it, the stone still felt solid.

It was as if a window had opened in the crown of the hill. When he looked down into it, he was astonished to see the living room of his own house below. The room was hazy with smoke, but he could see the fire flickering in the grate and the Bone Man leaning over someone on the couch.

Jonah hammered on the invisible stone. "Hey! I'm lost up here! You've got to help me!"

He was sure he had opened his mouth. He was sure he had shouted. But the words didn't come out right. They sounded different. Distant. As if they had been spoken by someone else, someone crying out in a dream.

He looked down and went cold. "No! No!"

Below, lying on the couch, he could see himself. His body. His face. His hands folded across his chest, the knuckles of his right hand bleeding.

The Bone Man stiffened as if he sensed Jonah watching. With one swift movement, he scooped up the bones and sent them cascading onto the floor in front of the fire. Jonah heard them tinkling clearly, like glass wind chimes, knocking together until eventually they fell still.

The Bone Man leaned forward, crouching as he picked through them, placing them in a circle according to some order only he knew. When all was ready, he took one last bone from the pouch—a bone without a symbol or marking of any sort—and placed it in the middle of the circle. Instantly, all the bones began to glow.

A moment later, a shaft of light shot up out of the hill into the sky. The sudden brightness caught Jonah by surprise and sent him reeling back. The light spotlighted the clouds above and immediately the stones around him began to glow too. They seemed to suck the light back out from the sky, feeding on its energy until they buzzed and crackled with it.

Jonah watched as dazzling rings of blue light ran up to the points of the stones and jumped off in lightning that struck at the air around him. He threw himself flat as the lightning zigzagged across the void, forming crooked spokes into the hub of light at the center. The brightness burned into the retinas of his eyes as the flashes wrote in laser images, projecting pictures in 3-D onto the screen of light. Images that left him in awe.

The pictures passed in machine-gun bursts. Some even too quick to see. His life flashed before his eyes as if he were drowning. He saw himself growing up surrounded by the faces and places he knew well, and yet at the same time, part of him always seemed to be somewhere else.

It was as if his life was overlaid with another's, like a negative of a film that had been doubly exposed with two images. Split. Divided. He was at home in Mulligan, but also in another place. A place he had never seen before in his life, but strangely knew equally well.

He recognized the house on the beachfront, the palm trees, and the way the white sand curved to meet a rocky point. He knew the lighthouse that overlooked the bay. The blue of the sea and sky did not startle him, nor did the brightness of the sunlight as it rode the surf in brilliant flashes. This place felt like home too.

He saw a girl coming toward him along the beach. She was about his age and he judged by her tan and the sun-bleached streaks in her long dark hair that she lived there. And as he watched her, he became aware of a feeling deep inside himself. A feeling of great calm. A calm he had never known before. As if somehow, just by seeing her, a circle had been made whole or a piece of him found that had been missing.

The 3-D image grew misty and faded.

"Wait! Please!" Jonah called out.

Too late. The girl was no more than a shape in the mist. Shadowy and indistinct. Distant.

"Who are you?" he whispered.

As he spoke, the light grew dimmer. Suddenly he saw a great storm approaching. The sky filled with purple-black clouds. The rain lashed down and bolts of fire stabbed out of the gloom like daggers. Then a hole opened in the darkness and a horde of demons came shrieking down, and with them came the Bone Man's giant face.

"Beware Edwin," the Bone Man's voice rolled with the thunder.

A demon with a pig's face dropped low and punched at Jonah. He flinched from the blow before realizing it was only another 3-D image.

When he looked up again, he saw only the demon's clawed hand floating in front of him. Its crooked fingers were spread wide as if trying to reach him. As he watched, the claw began to wither. The skin shriveled. The flesh fell away in rags to reveal the bones beneath. Then even these crumbled away to dust, until only one remained: a small bone, carved with a strange symbol and dyed in blood.

Jonah shot out of the long, dark tunnel into the light. Air rushed into his lungs as if he had held his breath to the extreme limit. He sat bolt upright, wide-eyed and staring.

It took a moment for him to realize he was on the couch. He guessed from the stiffness in his back and shoulders that he had been lying there for some time. He collected his thoughts and looked about him.

The fire was out and the ashes were gray and fragile in the grate. The front door was bolted on the inside. Somewhere in the brightness outside a blackbird was calling a warning across the garden. According to the clock on the mantelpiece it was 7:20 A.M.

"The Bone Man!" he remembered suddenly.

The Bone Man had gone.

The kitchen was deserted, the back door open. He looked around the garden, walking around to the front of the house to look up and down the lane. The Bone Man had vanished and had taken his things with him.

Jonah went back to the kitchen and sat down, leaning forward and resting his forehead on the table, cooling his brow on the plastic top.

"It couldn't have been a dream, could it?"

He started to thump his head on the table. Softly at first, then harder, until the cottage was filled with the dull thud of bone on wood. He ground his teeth and balled his fists, trying to drive the broken thoughts from his head.

"I...am...not...crazy!" he said and realized he was talking to himself, which was supposed to be a sign of mental illness. He groaned.

The mailbox snapped open. Brown envelopes tumbled onto the mat by the front door. Jonah glanced at the pile the postman had left.

"Just in time," his father said as he climbed down the creaking ladder. He scooped the letters from the floor. "I need some paper."

He hadn't shaved and the front of his shirt was dirty and stained. He scuffed through the kitchen with hardly a glance in Jonah's direction.

"Have you seen the Bone—er, I mean, Jack this morning?" Jonah asked hopefully.

"Jack? No."

"I think he's gone."

His father shrugged then noticed the bruises on Jonah's face. "Hope the other fella looks worse," he growled and turned away.

Jonah rested his forehead on the table again but looked up a moment later. His father hadn't moved. He was staring at one of the letters. The letter looked different from the rest. The envelope was blue, not the usual brown of the bills.

"Is it bad news, Dad?"

His father seemed startled. He gave Jonah a wild-eyed look, glanced down at the letter again, then hurriedly stuffed it into his pocket.

"It's nothing. Just forget it," he said, then added, "Aren't you supposed to be in school?" He disappeared into the garden. A moment later, the wooden door of the outside toilet slammed shut.

The news must have been bad, Jonah thought.

He climbed up the ladder to his room, threw himself on his bed, and stared at the ceiling. He thought about the Bone Man and wondered why he had gone in the night without a word.

A thought popped into Jonah's head and he sat up suddenly. He glanced toward the old dresser in the corner. The long drawer in the bottom was open slightly. His heart started beating faster. He knelt on the floor. The drawer was broken and wouldn't slide open far. He reached in and dug through the jumble of clothes and blankets until he touched metal. His fingers closed around the rectangular shape of the tin and he pulled it out.

It was an old tea box with "Starbright's Tea" printed on the lid. Inside, Jonah kept all the small things he prized most in the world. He wrenched off the lid and looked in.

The photo of his mother was still there. Relieved, he took it out and checked it carefully. It was a creased fragment of time, frozen forever like the smile on her face. She was standing at the door of White Bird Cottage cradling Jonah in her arms, a small baby in blue. It was the only picture he had ever seen of her and it was more precious to him than all the rest put together: his grandfather's knife, his diver's watch, the sports cards, and even the money he had saved over the years by helping Fergus on the Sligo Queen.

Jonah took out the little bundle of cash and counted it. There wasn't much, but it was all there, along with some coins. He was about to put the lid back when he noticed something else in the bottom of the tin. He shook up the contents and pulled out a small, carved bone.

"It can't be!"

But it was.

Jonah's mind raced through the events of the previous night as he remembered them, but his thoughts jolted against the memory of the stones. It must have been a dream. And yet here was the bone with the same strange symbol carved on it:

Then he remembered falling over the flat stone in the center of the stone circle. He thought for a moment before slowly raising his right hand. He stared at the blood drying on his knuckles.

*

"It was a dream, Jonah! Just a stupid dream." Megan shut her locker in a way that was meant to indicate that these were her final words on the matter.

"Then how do you explain this?" Jonah said. He pulled the bone from his pocket, holding it out between his thumb and forefinger.

She glanced at it briefly and shrugged. "How do I know? I mean, you might have found it or even carved it yourself."

"And why would I want to do that?"

"I don't know," she sounded exasperated, "maybe to prove you're right or something."

She spun on her heel and walked away.

"But Meg!" Jonah went after her. The only reason he had come to school was to talk to her about what had happened. "I know you're angry about the book and I'm sorry," he said, "but please, Meg—you have to believe me!"

"I don't have to do anything you say, Jonah."

"But—"

"Don't you see? I've had enough, Jonah, enough! I know it isn't easy for you at home, but all this stuff you keep going on about—it's too weird, Jonah!"

"I know it sounds that way, Meg, but it's true." He thought quickly. "Look!" He held out his right hand. "My knuckles are still bleeding from when I scraped them on that stone."

Meg rolled her eyes. "Jonah! You did that down at Craxkull Point. I was there, remember? Which reminds me, you lost my handkerchief down at Craxkull."

"Forget the handkerchief! I was—"

"Dreaming!" she snapped. "It all just happened inside your head, Jonah! Inside your head!"

"But what about the girl? It was her, you know—I'm sure of it."

"Oh yes, the girl," Megan said, her green eyes flashing suddenly. "Why don't you tell me all about her again?"

Jonah missed the sarcasm in her voice and thought she meant it. "Well, it's hard to say, but I know she was tall and had long hair," he said. "Oh, I don't know. She looked awesome, nothing like any of the girls around here."

"Is that so?" Megan folded her arms, tapping out her irritation on the floor with her foot.

"And the weirdest part of all," he went on, missing all the danger signs, "is that I feel like I've known her forever."

"Well, if you ask me, Jonah Ebbers," Megan started in a quiet voice that grew suddenly louder, "whoever she is, she's welcome to you! Now, if you don't mind, I'm going to class, even if you're not." She turned and stormed down the hallway.

Jonah could only stand and watch as she pushed through the door into Mr. Morran's class. He hovered around outside for a short while in the hope she might come back out, then decided to go home. Unfortunately, he bumped straight into Mr. Morran.

"Glad to see you're feeling better, Jonah," his teacher said, catching him by the arm. He frowned at the bruises on Jonah's face. "Megan Doherty said you were ill—I didn't realize you'd had an accident too."

"It's nothing," Jonah said.

"Is that so? Well, maybe we should have a little chat about it anyway," Mr. Morran said, steering Jonah into the classroom. He ignored Jonah's feeble protests and smiled. "But first I want to find out just how much you know about the great Roman Empire."

Not a lot, was the answer to that.

The test (much like the rest of the day) dragged on. Jonah sat in front of a blank page without a hope of answering any of the questions. He didn't care much. The future seemed more important than the past. So he studied the bone under the desk, turning it between the tips of his fingers so the strange symbol caught the light:

He wondered if it was some kind of black magic. After all, he knew the Bone Man had strange powers. How else could he have known about the tin hidden in the drawer? But if Jonah wasn't certain of much, he was sure of one thing—finding the bone with the money proved the Bone Man hadn't been out to rob them.

He remembered the Bone Man's warning.

Beware Edwin.

His thoughts raced, jumbling up and leaving him feeling slightly sick.

He shifted uncomfortably in his chair and glanced around the class, studying each face in turn before noticing Mr. Morran was watching him. He ducked back over his test paper. No Edwins there. Unless...he gave his teacher a suspicious look.

"A word with you, Jonah, if you don't mind," Mr. Morran said as the class ended and they handed in their test papers.

Jonah dodged the general rush for the door and approached Mr. Morran's desk cautiously.

"I'd like to have that little chat with you now," Mr. Morran said, his tone casual, his eyes quick.

Jonah was suspicious. "What about?"

"Well, about you being absent so much, for a start. Then there are those bruises." A pause followed. He chose his words carefully. "I hear your father has been drinking again."

"That's a lie! He's given it up for good."

"Well, I'm glad to hear it, but all the same those bruises—"

"I got them surfing!"

"I see," Mr. Morran said, still looking. He seemed unconvinced. "Nevertheless, I think I should talk with your father. Nothing serious. Just about how you're doing, that sort of thing. I'm always willing to help in any way I can. You only have to ask."

"We don't need any help," Jonah said bluntly.

Mr. Morran opened a file and pulled out an envelope. "All the same, would you give this note to your father when you get home? Don't forget, now. It's important."

Jonah took the envelope by the corner as if the contents were poisoned. He nodded and left Mr. Morran cleaning the chalkboard.

Later, Jonah sat on the bus. It was crowded, but the seat next to his remained empty. Across the aisle, he saw Billy tap one of the Gallagher girls on the shoulder. She nudged her sister. They all shot sidelong glances in his direction, then looked away quickly.

Jonah ignored them and looked out of the window at the flat-fronted classrooms. He tried not to think of Megan, who was sitting with Martin O'Leary at the back. The doors shut with a hiss and the bus pulled away. He watched the streets slide by, wishing the journey was over.

By the time the bus pulled in under the branches of the old oak by Gallagher's farm, Jonah was feeling awkward. He was sure everyone was talking about him behind his back.

He stood up and ignored the complaints as he elbowed his way off the bus first. Then he set off up the lane to the gate into Gallagher's field. He climbed over the gate, dropped his backpack into the hedge and set off again across the field. He broke into a run as he approached the cliffs. His feet thumped into the path and he ran without stopping until he reached Craxkull Point.

*

Jonah sat on the cliff with his legs dangling over the drop. The sea was spread out before him, its cold greenness flecked with whitecaps, widening to the horizon where it blurred with the sky and came hurtling back overhead, magically transformed into shades of gray.

He reached into his pocket and pulled out Mr. Morran's note, pinching it between his thumb and forefinger so it flapped in the breeze. He was tempted to let it go, but he knew there would be another note, and one after that too. He wouldn't be allowed to ignore them. He had learned that much the last time they had tried to take him into foster care.

He slipped his finger under the flap of the envelope and tested the strength of the glue. He loosened it a little and it opened without tearing.

Sure enough, it was bad news. Mr. Morran expressed his deep concerns about Jonah. About him missing school. About the bruises. About the rumors that his father was drinking again. The note suggested a meeting as soon as possible in order that the matter could be discussed. It was signed Patrick Morran and dated on the bottom.

Jonah read the name, sighed, stuffed the letter back in the envelope, then the envelope back in his pocket. As he did, his fingers touched the bone and he immediately thought about the Bone Man's warning again.

"But I don't know any Edwins," he said and stood up.

As he looked down, he could see the white birds flying sorties from the cliffs below, dipping and rising on the wind, soaring above the waves that fell heavily on Skullcrack. He wondered what it would be like to fly with them. Escape. He spread his arms wide, closed his eyes, and drank in the salty breeze, imagining.

As he let his thoughts fly, his mind seemed to stretch. His eyes were still closed, but he found he was able to see right through the lids. The sky on the other side was suddenly no longer gray—it was blue—and he saw a streak of light. A bright flare climbing steadily, powering upward, trailing a plume of smoke like a huge, puffed flower.

He opened his eyes and instantly the image vanished as his thoughts snapped back inside his head. Everything was as it had been before. Confused, he scanned the sky for any sign of the dazzling light and as he did, he swayed dangerously close to the edge. The drop tripped his eye, set his head spinning and dragged his gaze down in a dizzying freefall.

"Don't do it!"

Jonah heard the shout, felt the hand on his collar, and a split-second later he was yanked sharply backward. The sky somersaulted. The white birds shrieked. He hit the ground and someone landed on him with his full weight, like a wrestler going in for the slam.

"Oh, very good, Macca!" another voice said. "Now you've gone and flattened the kid!"

"But you said he was gonna jump," the one called Macca said, holding Jonah down with his weight. "What was I supposed to do?"

"I said talk him out of it, man, not bust his head!"

"Gee-zuz, I was only trying to save the kid's life!" Macca said. "I'd get a medal or something for doing that back home."

"I can't breathe," Jonah gasped.

A pause. They looked at him.

"You heard him, Macca! The kid can't breathe!"

The weight lifted off him and Jonah doubled up. The one called Macca—the big one with the long hair tied back in a ponytail—threatened to land on him again, just as hard, if he so much as looked at the edge.

"I wasn't going to jump," Jonah said when he had gasped back some of his breath.

"See! What did I tell you," the one that wasn't Macca said. He had short dark hair and the thin wisps of a goatee on the point of his chin. He thumped Macca's shoulder. "The kid wasn't even going to jump and you nearly killed him, man!"

"But you said he was."

"Sorry about that, kid. My friend Macca here got the wrong end of the boomerang as usual," he said. Goatee Beard helped Jonah to his feet, introducing himself as Eddie.

Jonah heard a shout and looked around to see someone making desperate efforts to prevent a graffiti-covered van rolling through the open gate into Gallagher's field. He could see surfboards attached to the roof along with camping gear.

Suddenly Eddie and Macca were shouting. "The sticks! Save the sticks!" They forgot all about Jonah and ran back to save their boards. "Use the emergency brake, Brown Cat! The emergency brake!"

They converged on the van and rammed their shoulders into the front to slow it down while the one they called Brown Cat jumped in and put on the brakes. The van rolled gently to a stop a few yards from the edge.

Once the van was stopped, an argument broke out about whose fault it was. Eddie and Macca chased Brown Cat all around the field, until eventually they all collapsed, laughing.

"This is Gallagher's field," Jonah pointed out as he approached them cautiously.

Eddie sat up. "Relax, man. The farmer said it was cool." He looked out over the sea. "We were heading for the surf up at Easky when we saw that lefthander down there from the road." He pointed toward Skullcrack. "Is that break something else or what! We were looking for a way down the cliff when we saw you."

"Still say I saved his life," Macca muttered.

They started unloading. Macca stood on top of the van and threw down the rolled-up tents.

Jonah was horrified. Skullcrack was his place. He didn't want to share it with anyone—least of all those three. He thought quickly.

"You're wasting your time," he said. "There isn't a way down to Skullcrack."

"So it's got a name then," Eddie said casually.

Jonah shrugged. "It's what the fishermen here call it. You're wasting your time."

They were all looking at him now.

"We'll be the ones to decide that," Brown Cat said. He looked at Eddie, who seemed to be their leader. "Right?"

Eddie nodded, but he wore a dangerous look. "You ain't holding out on us, are you?"

"No way! I swear."

"That's good," Eddie said, "because it would be a dumb kid who came between us and surf like that, right Brown Cat?"

Brown Cat made a strange rumbling noise in his throat, sounding more like a bear than a cat.

Jonah backed away, turned, and ran across the field. He stopped at the hedge to grab his books, then ran out into the lane.

When he looked back, Eddie was watching him.

The deck of the Sligo Queen moved gently under Jonah's feet as they rounded the point. They turned three points to starboard, their wake describing the turn in a curve of white water, and began the run back to Mulligan with the seagulls strung out at intervals behind them.

They had been out since dawn, but the catch that Saturday had been poor. Some mackerel, half a dozen lobsters from the pots near Lenadoon and the usual crabs. Fergus stood silently at the wheel in the wheelhouse. Brooding. Listening to the weather forecast crackling on the radio as he steered their course for home.

Jonah looked out over the starboard rail, watching the rugged coastline slip by, hoping the poor catch would not cut his pay. His gaze surfed the waves breaking on Craxkull Point. His spirits lifted when he saw no surfers, but sank again when he picked out the orange and blue patches of the tents pitched in Gallagher's field.

Three days had passed since Eddie and the others had pitched their tents on Craxkull Point. Three days of some of the best surf Jonah had ever seen, and yet he had been unable to go anywhere near Skullcrack. Each day he had looked out hopefully. Each day he had seen the smoke from their campfire rising above the hedges in a thin line and unfurling in the breeze like a flag. It was as if Gallagher's field had been occupied by an enemy. Invaders who had come to steal and plunder what was rightfully his.

But the hidden path had remained a secret.

They had paddled around Craxkull Point on their boards, but they had been beaten back by the waves. Undeterred, they had attempted the approach from the giant rocks of Gorag's Hurl and had been caught by the fierce rip that had sent so many ships to their doom.

"There's no telling some people," Fergus had said, shaking his head.

Without Skullcrack, Jonah felt as if he had been thrown into the wilderness. The one thing he had always been sure of had suddenly been taken from him. He felt cheated. Lost. His head was constantly full of broken thoughts and he was now at the total mercy of the demons of White Bird Cottage.

At night, in the dark of his room, they tormented him ceaselessly with their whisperings. Questions, questions, always questions. Who was the girl? Why did he keep seeing things that weren't there? Why did a place he had never seen before feel like home? And why had the Bone Man left so much unanswered? But most of all, they asked about Edwin.

Eddie, Macca, and Brown Cat had not escaped their attention either:

Eddie? That has to be short for ssssomething.

Yes, sssomething, the others always agreed.

Edward? Edgar? Eddison?
Edwin!

They left Jonah feeling cold.

The roar of the diesel engine dropped to idle as they navigated the narrow harbor entrance, slipping between the stone jaws with the harbor lights to port and starboard. Men with fishing rods watched stoically as they passed. The gap of green water narrowed until the rubber tires on the side of the Sligo Queen rubbed up against the stone. The engine died as Jonah jumped onto the dock to hook the ropes to the hooks, securing the boat bow and stern.

Together they stacked the boxes of fish on the dock, then Jonah hosed down the deck, chasing pieces of fish with the jet of water. Once the ropes and deck gear had been stowed, he picked up his things from the wheelhouse and hung around Fergus.

"Here," Fergus said in Gaelic as he dipped into his trouser pocket. He leafed off two bills from a thin roll of money. Paused. Glanced at Jonah. Leafed off another fiver and slapped the money into Jonah's eager hands. "And there's a bit extra so you can buy yourself something proper to eat —you look half starved."

Jonah thanked him until Fergus told him to stop. He didn't want people to think he'd gone soft in his old age. "*Slán, Jonah!*" he said and settled down to mend a broken winch.

"*Slán agat!*" Jonah answered and they parted.

Jonah did not look at The Crooked Finger as he turned the corner and started up the hill. He could feel the pig-beast's presence radiating out of the place like heat. He turned his back on it and thrust his hands deep into his pockets, one hand closed tight around the money while the other found the bone and Mr. Morran's note.

He decided he couldn't put off the moment much longer. He would have to give his father the note sometime. He made up his mind to leave it on the kitchen table that night for him to find. The hill seemed steeper than usual, the lane longer as he made his way home, all the while wondering what would happen and hoping his father hadn't been drinking again.

*

It was just after 5 when Jonah arrived home.
"Dad?" he called as he came in the back way.
Silence.

He kicked the back door closed behind him, made his usual rummage of the fridge in the hope of finding something to eat, then scuffed through to the living room where he dumped his stuff on the chair. The fire took some minutes to start. The greedy little flames devoured the sticks and made him feel hungrier than ever.

Jonah switched on the television. It hummed noisily as it warmed up and the picture jumped and scrolled crazily. He slammed his fist down on the top and the jumping slowed and stopped. Satisfied, he dropped into the couch and put his feet up, waiting for the sports scores, drifting through the news reports until his attention was caught briefly by a report on NASA's recent launch from Cape Canaveral:

"5...4...3...2...1. Ignition. We have green for engine go!" The announcer's voice lifted with the rocket, engines flaring in the square of sky.

The picture started jumping frantically again and Jonah was too busy thumping the top of the old set to notice the way the rocket streaked up into the sky trailing a plume of smoke behind it.

No matter how hard he hit the set, the picture wouldn't settle so he gave up and turned it off. He lay down on the couch and stared moodily at the blank screen, then gazed up at the bookshelves and their books. He read some of the titles, remembering something the Bone Man had said. About learning a lot about people from the books they read. It occurred to Jonah that his mother had probably read most, if not all, of the books on the shelves in front of him.

"Take my advice," his father had said on one of the few occasions he had talked about Jonah's mother. "Stay away from books. Your mother used to read all the time and look where it got her!" Drunk, he often threatened to burn them. Sober, he never did.

Intrigued, Jonah wondered if somewhere in those yellowing pages she had left clues about herself just like the Bone Man said. He stood up and ran his finger over dusty sounding names.

Dickens, Tolstoy, and Tolkien...until he reached one which, for a reason he couldn't remember, seemed familiar: W. B. Yeats. It was a book of poetry. He blew off the dust. The spine cracked as he opened it, and he saw that someone had written something in pen on the inside of the cover.

> To Marie,
>
> I would that we were, my beloved, white birds on the foam of the sea!
>
> W.

Jonah recognized it as his father's clumsy handwriting and read the inscription again. The words sounded soft, not at all like the father he knew.

Jonah put the book on the arm of the chair and started flicking through the others. One after the other. Riffling through the pages as if he expected all the clues to be obvious. They weren't, of course. The things that had made his mother laugh or cry were hidden in a million words. Disappointed, he was about to give up when something slipped from the top of the last book in the line and fell, tinkling on the floor.

Puzzled, he picked it up, holding it in the flat of his hand. It was a small key. He glanced around, trying to think of something in White Bird Cottage worth locking.

"Like a locked box," he murmured. "That was what the Bone Man said."

Jonah looked at the wooden chest beneath the window. He hadn't paid it much attention before.

It had always just been there, low and squat by the front door, a crumbling antique, deposited there in passing. Jonah quickly knelt to see if the key fitted the lock. Sure enough, the key turned smoothly and the lid came open without a sound.

Later, Jonah wondered what he had expected to find in there. Some long forgotten family treasure, perhaps? Whatever it was, when he first saw the bundle of papers and assorted junk inside, he was disappointed.

At first, it was the letter in the blue envelope that caught his eye. He recognized it immediately as the one that had arrived a few days before. It was on top of four or five letters tied up with string. Each had been addressed to a post office box in Dublin and forwarded to his father. The sender's name and address were clearly marked on the back of them all: Sally Dayton, Storm Island, Florida, USA. All were dated by the postmarks. The oldest was more than a year old. All had been kept carefully. And all were unopened.

Curious, Jonah was wondering how he could open one without it showing when he noticed something else. He delved deeper into the box and suddenly there it was: the photograph.

The photo was so similar to the one of his mother cradling him in her arms that at first he thought somehow his father had found it. But when he looked closer, he saw that it was different. It was as if the photograph had been taken shortly before or after his. But there was something more than just a different pose, something he couldn't quite put his finger on.

He decided the letters could wait while he compared the two photographs. He was careful to put everything back the way it had been. Only when the chest was locked, the key back on the book, and everything looked as it had, did Jonah take the photo up to his room.

His hands were trembling as he pulled out the tin, spilling the contents on the floor in his hurry. Fumbling, he placed the two photographs side by side, only to be immediately disappointed. It was nothing more than a difference in the color of the clothes: in one, Jonah was dressed in blue baby clothes; in the other, red.

However, the consolation of having two photographs of his mother where before he had one, outweighed everything else. As he looked at her, he found himself wishing he could be that baby again just so he could feel her arms around him. He longed to bury his face in her clothes and breathe in her warmth. Suddenly he was filled with an overwhelming sense of his loss. It seemed to grip him and squeeze until he ached.

He was so busy wishing, he didn't hear the motorcycle coming up the lane or the slam of the back door as his father came home.

"Are you there, Jo?"

Startled, Jonah looked up.

The ladder creaked.

Jonah's heart raced. The tin, the photos, the money, everything was spread out on the floor.

He scooped it all up, crammed it back into the tin, and slammed on the lid. He had just enough time to hide the tin in the drawer, but the drawer stuck as he pushed it back in. He was still on his knees fighting with it when his father walked in.

"Dad! It's you!" Jonah said, sounding too loud and breathless.

"Who'd you expect, the Pope?" his father said, glancing at the drawer. His eyes narrowed.

" 'Course not." Jonah stood up and quickly moved away from the drawer.

His father grinned. "And what've you got hidden in that closet, Jo? A skeleton, is it?"

"No. Nothing!"

His father dragged his gaze from the drawer. He frowned, thought for a moment as if trying to recall exactly what had brought him up there, then remembered: "I need some money, Jo."

"What for?"

His father didn't answer him directly. "It's Saturday. Fergus must have paid you, right?"

Jonah couldn't easily deny it. "Yes, but—"

"Fish and chips."

"Fish and chips?"

"You asked me what I wanted it for. Fish and chips. For our supper. You'd like that, wouldn't you?"

"Everyone likes fish and chips," Jonah replied, wondering if he'd forgotten his own birthday.

His father nodded. "Thought I'd go down to Finnegan's and pick some up. Only I'm clean out." His father patted the pockets of his jacket. He shot a shifty look at Jonah. "So will you lend me some, Jo?"

Jonah reached into his pocket for the money Fergus had just given him, paused, and looked at his father suspiciously. "You're not thinking of going down to The Crooked Finger, are you?"

His father swore the thought had never crossed his mind.

Jonah sighed. "I haven't got much."

"It'll do," his father said, snatching it from his hand. "And don't worry, I'll pay you back." He counted it and seemed disappointed at how little there was. "I'll have to have a word with that Fergus," he growled.

His gaze flicked back to the drawer and lingered there for a moment longer than it should have. But he said nothing and when he left, he promised to bring back double portions of chips.

Jonah placed Mr. Morran's note carefully against the ketchup bottle, looked at it critically, then snatched it away again, and stuffed it back into his pocket. He didn't want to spoil a good fish supper with his father. Bad news could wait.

It was getting dark outside. His father had been away for some time and Jonah was expecting him back from Finnegan's Fish Shop at any moment. He hoped he would hurry. He was so hungry he was feeling dizzy, and the thought of fish and chips made his mouth water.

He had scrubbed the table, set the knives and forks, and was sitting in his place, ready. He considered himself lucky that his father hadn't seen the photographs or the tin. Okay, so he had lost the money, but Fergus had given him the extra so he could eat properly and he decided it would be worth it if it meant being with his dad.

He was thinking about the letters in the wooden chest and listening for the motorcycle in the lane when he heard someone opening the front gate instead. The hinges were rusty and sang a flat note as the gate opened and closed. A pause. And suddenly a knock came at the door.

"What do you want?" Jonah asked, when he opened the door and found Billy standing on the front doorstep.

Billy looked startled and backed off on the path. "I—I—I—"

"Where's Meg?"

"She's not here."

"I can see that!"

Billy recovered a little of his composure. "She sent me with a message," he said, fidgeting.

"A message?" Jonah looked at him.

"Yes, she said, 'Give Jonah Ebbers this message, because I'm not going to go anywhere near him.' " He nodded, looking pleased with himself. "That's what she said."

Any hope that Megan might have forgiven him died. Jonah sighed, "And?"

"And," Billy said, suddenly remembering there was more, "she said to tell you that Mr. Morran was at our house earlier, asking questions about you." Billy's eyes grew wide. "I didn't say nothing about your dad beating you, honest."

Jonah glared at him. "What sort of questions?"

Billy couldn't remember exactly, but he said it didn't matter because Mr. Morran had said he would ask Jonah himself. "When he comes over later."

It took a moment for Jonah to realize the full importance of the message. "Mr. Morran is coming here to see me?"

"Later," Billy added, for complete accuracy.

"Later? But that's now!"

"Hey! My sister only paid me to deliver the message. She didn't say anything about when!" Having delivered it, Billy made his escape to the other side of the front gate.

There, he paused and looked back. "Oh, and by the way, you're wasting your time with her. Megan won't talk to you. She thinks you're crazy. I heard her say so."

And with that he was gone, running back down the lane to Mulligan.

*

"Bloody, nosy, do-gooder teachers!" Jonah snarled as he slammed the front door.

He looked around at the mess. The cottage hadn't been cleaned for months and he had to make it look like the best, cleanest, happiest home in all of County Sligo.

Jonah knew what would happen if Mr. Morran wasn't happy with what he saw. They had been through it all before. Mr. Morran would tell the principal at school; the principal would talk to "nice" Miss Fingle. Before long the whole place would be swarming with people from the social services, saying they wanted to help him.

"We don't need anyone's help!" he hissed at his own reflection in the mirror above the fireplace. His image was split by a crack in the glass. "We'll show them. We're just as good as anyone else around here!"

He started with the refrigerator. They'll look in there to see if I'm eating properly, he thought to himself. He scooped out the old packages and pizza crusts, arranged the jars so the ones that looked the moldiest were at the back, and wiped everything as clean as he could using hot water from the kettle. They had run out of milk, so he filled the carton with water from the tap to make it feel full and put it back in. He stood back. If anything, the fridge looked emptier.

He racked his brains, trying to imagine what a full one might contain: cheese, eggs, fish, bread.

Cheese was easy. He took off his shoe without untying the laces and put it in an old plastic bag, knotting the neck of the bag so that it looked like a wedge. Smooth stones from outside the back door soon became eggs in a carton. A shirt was transformed into a piece of fish wrapped up in newspaper and tied up with string. He threw away the crusts in the bag of bread and replaced them with a sponge from under the sink. It felt squeezably fresh. Then he stood back to see how it all looked. The thought of all that food made his mouth water.

He cleaned up the rest of the house as best he could. He remembered the light was broken in the living room and swapped the bulb for one from his room. The place had started to look respectable. Satisfied, he sat down to wait.

In the shadows above, the demons of White Bird Cottage stirred. Jonah could feel their eyes on him. They were watching him through the trapdoor, hanging back just out of the light where the shadows were deepest, peeping around the ladder. Whispering.

Where's hisssss father then? one asked.

Not here, that's for ssssssure, another agreed.

Been gone a while.

With the money too.

They nodded and nudged one another. *The Crooked Finger is close to Finnegan's Fish Shop.*

So clossssse.

They came to the same conclusion at once. *Yes, the boy's trusting. So trussssssssting.*

They goaded Jonah to his feet. "Just shut up! Shut up!"

He scaled the ladder and switched on every light he could. The demons wailed and gnashed their teeth, scuttling about as they looked for places dark enough to hide, until eventually they crammed themselves behind the closet and Jonah slammed the door on their fury.

He was still breathing hard when Mr. Morran knocked at the door.

*

"Hope you don't mind me dropping in like this, Jonah," Mr. Morran said. "Is your father home?"

"He's gone for fish and chips."

"I don't mind waiting," Mr. Morran said, stepping in without being invited. He hung his cap on the hook by the door in a way that left Jonah in no doubt he meant to stay.

"He could be gone a while," Jonah said.

Mr. Morran said he didn't mind. Anyway, it would give them a chance for a little chat.

"That'll be good," Jonah said, rolling his eyes.

Mr. Morran looked around and started complimenting Jonah on what he saw: "Always liked this house. Just the right size. That ladder is a bit dangerous, though. Nice fire." He chatted about those sort of things until he ran out of small talk and sat down to warm himself by the fire.

Silence.

"Fish and chips, you say?" Mr. Morran broke it. Jonah nodded.

Another silence, even more awkward.

Jonah's hand automatically went to the note in his pocket. He pushed it down deeper. His hand found the bone and he pulled it out, fingering it nervously. The idea of his father coming home and meeting Mr. Morran was not a pleasant one.

"Maybe you should come back tomorrow." Jonah tried to shake off Mr. Morran.

"I don't mind waiting, Jonah," Mr. Morran insisted. "Really I don't." He remembered a bar of chocolate he had in his pocket and pulled it out. *Tá ocras ort, is dócha?*

Jonah shook his head and said he wasn't hungry. But he couldn't help looking at the chocolate. It reminded him just how hungry he was. He had to be careful, though. It could be some sort of trick dreamed up by Mr. Morran to see if he was eating properly. No, he would lie, he wasn't hungry at all.

"We've got loads of food here," he said, and startled Mr. Morran by insisting that he see for himself. He opened the fridge door with a flourish. "See—it's stuffed."

"That cheese smells good," Mr. Morran agreed. "And you're right, I suppose, you shouldn't spoil your appetite if your dad's bringing home fish and chips." He put the chocolate back in his pocket as they went to sit by the fire again. Mr. Morran picked up the book lying on the arm of the chair. He looked impressed. "You never told me you liked W. B. Yeats, Jonah."

"Who?" Jonah looked puzzled, then remembered the book of poetry. "Oh him! Yeah, me and my dad like him the best."

A dreamy look came into Mr. Morran's eye. "Ah Yeats," he said, "one of County Sligo's most famous poets."

Mr. Morran put on his glasses—they were round and wire-rimmed—and opened the book. He read the hand-written inscription aloud, " 'To Marie, I would that we were, my beloved, white birds on the foam of the sea! W.' " Mr. Morran glanced at Jonah. "It's part of Yeats' poem 'The White Birds,' " he said and recited the whole poem from memory. He finished and looked at Jonah. "Marie was your mother's name?"

Jonah nodded, turning the bone in his fingers.

More silence. Mr. Morran glanced around as if he expected to see the ghost of Marie Ebbers standing behind him and put down the book quickly. He noticed the bone and seemed pleased to be able to change the subject.

"A rune bone," Mr. Morran said as he squinted at the strange symbol scratched on the bone.

It was Jonah's turn to be surprised. "You mean you've seen marks like this before?"

"We studied Celtic Runes and the Ogham in history, remember?"

"History?"

"Yes, you know, that waste of good surfing time we have on Mondays and Thursdays."

Jonah felt the blood hot in his face. "I didn't mean...er...what I meant was, what's history got to do with this bone?"

"Maybe if you were in class more often you'd find out," Mr. Morran said. He sighed and shook his head. "Just about everything that happens today is caused by something that happened in the past. You don't have to look far into Irish history to see that. Take the Troubles in the North, for example. They go back hundreds of years. But what happened then, and since then, still affects what goes on today." He nodded as if this alone proved his point. "Oh yes, history makes the present all right and it shapes the future."

"Yes, but what about the bone?" Jonah asked. "It's some sort of weird magic, right?"

Mr. Morran laughed and shook his head. Runes were a sort of ancient writing, he explained, and each one meant something. "This symbol, I know well," he said pointing:

"It's part of the Rune Poem."

"You mean like R. and W. B. Yeats's poems?"

"Sort of, but the Rune Poem is much older. Well over a thousand years older. There are twenty-nine verses in all, and each has a runic symbol. This is the last one. The twenty-ninth:

" 'We hate the clay, the cold flesh,
the pale corpse, the fallen
flowers, the broken promise.' "

"It has a name, *Ear.* Some say it means Clay. Others," he paused, "Death." He looked at Jonah.

"Where did you get this?"

"I found it." It was only half a lie.

"It's probably very old then—even though it doesn't look it," Mr. Morran said, clearly surprised by the bone. "If you had been a Celt living in Ireland all those years ago and you'd been given one of these, you'd have been very worried. You see, back then they believed in the *aes dana*—the gifted ones. They were mystical people a bit like druids and were said to have supernatural powers."

Jonah listened with growing unease as Mr. Morran told him that these gifted ones were renowned for their ability to see into the future by reading the runes. And (as if that wasn't enough) how they were supposed to be able to make spirit journeys. This they did by putting someone in a trance and leading their spirit to another place and time, so that person could make contact with both the living and the dead.

"Even great kings believed in their powers enough not to fight battles if the *aes dana* saw ill omens in the runes," Mr. Morran said. "It's my guess this bone was just that—an ill omen or warning of some kind." He turned it over in his fingers. "It would have been given to someone along with a warning about a place or a name."

"Beware Edwin," Jonah murmured.

Mr. Morran nodded. "Something like that."

Suddenly Jonah felt very lonely. "And these people—do they still exist?"

"The *aes dana*? Who knows. It depends if you believe that some people have powers science cannot explain. Personally, I don't," Mr. Morran said, handing back the bone and glancing at his watch. He frowned. It was almost 8 o'clock. "Your father has been a very long time."

"Maybe Finnegan's ran out of fish," Jonah said.

"There has to be a first time for everything, I suppose," Mr. Morran said, "but there'd be some who'd say it would be difficult—being down there on the harbor with all those fishing boats coming and going."

Half an hour later, Mr. Morran stood up. "I've obviously come on a bad night," he said, in a tone that sounded as if he thought every night would be the same. "Will you tell your father I called and remind him about my note? It's important I speak to him before school on Monday."

Jonah was only too happy to say goodbye.

Mr. Morran paused at the door, cap in hand. He glanced down at Jonah's bare feet, thought for a moment, then pulled out the chocolate bar again. "Here, you'd better have this," he said. "After all, I wouldn't want you to have to eat that shoe of yours in the fridge."

Two hours later, Wex Ebbers returned. Jonah heard the sound of his motorcycle in the lane and watched him through the window as he parked by the garage and then staggered around to the back door. He didn't have any fish and chips.

"I didn't have enough money," he growled, dropping heavily into the chair by the fire.

He produced a bottle of Old Agony from the pocket of his leather jacket. The new seal cracked as he twisted off the cap.

"What are you staring at?" he snarled, swigging down several gulps of the brown spirit. Judging by the look on his face, it hurt.

As the fiery spirit burned down into his stomach, his father's face contorted. His eyes disappeared into tiny slits. His lips twisted out of shape. And for one fleeting moment, Jonah saw the pig-beast's face leering back at him.

He backed away in horror and fled out through the back door into the night.

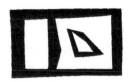

"Megan! Pssst! Megan!" Jonah threw a pebble at her window. It rattled on the glass, then pattered down through the ivy to land at his feet.

The window remained dark.

He called again as loud as he dared. More pebbles—more rattling and pattering. Still nothing.

The clock on Mulligan's church tower marked the quarter hour with a single bell note, a mournful sound on the chill of midnight. A dog barked somewhere on the other side of the village.

Jonah had been outside the Dohertys' house for more than an hour, hiding in the bushes by the front gate. Watching. Waiting. Wondering what to do. He had been able to see through a gap in the curtains into their front room. Every once in a while he caught fleeting glimpses of Megan as she moved about. It seemed an eternity before she went upstairs to bed.

When her bedroom light went on, Jonah had made up his mind. He had left the safety of the bushes and crept across the lawn to the corner of the house. He had called out to her as she came to close the curtains, but she hadn't heard. A moment later, the curtains had shut him out.

He had called over and over. From the cover of the ivy, Jonah had watched as Mr. Doherty opened the door and stood on the step.

"Who's there?" he had growled, scratching the bulge of his stomach. He had stood like that for a while before going back inside.

After that, Jonah had waited until everyone had gone to bed.

As he listened to the church clock striking, he decided he had waited long enough. He picked up some more pebbles, discarded the bigger stones so he wouldn't crack the windowpane, and then hurled them into the shadows above his head. They crackled and smacked against the glass, cascading down through the ivy.

Megan's light came on and the curtains opened. A moment later the window went sliding up and she looked down, her hair falling around her face. "Who's there?" she whispered.

"It's me!"

She peered into the darkness. "Jonah?"

"Keep your voice down or your dad'll hear." He paused, listening, but no other lights came on.

They spoke in whispers after that.

"For pete's sake, Jonah—it's almost 1 o'clock in the morning!"

"I know. I'm sorry, but I have to talk to you."

"It's too late for that, Jonah!"

Before he could stop her, she had ducked back inside. The window came sliding down and the curtains closed him out once more.

Jonah called but she wouldn't answer, so he tugged at the ivy, testing its strength. It was old and matted and reached all the way to the gutters of the roof. He guessed it was strong enough to hold his weight.

After one false start, he was climbing quickly. Hand over hand, snaking his way up through the waxy leaves until he reached her window. He found a hold and perched there, his shoulders level with the window ledge. He reached out and knocked gently. The light was quick to come on this time—as if Megan had been expecting something to happen—and the curtains flew open.

"I told you to leave me alone!" she hissed, opening the window a little.

"But Meg! Please!"

His foot slipped and he searched blindly for another toehold without much success. He made a lunge for the windowsill and held on.

"If my father finds you hanging outside my bedroom window he'll go ballistic," she said, glancing nervously over her shoulder. "Please! Just go!"

She was so worried about her father, she didn't notice his fingers hooked onto the windowsill. Suddenly the window was guillotining down. He pulled his hand away just in time.

The window flew away from him with Megan's face still framed behind the glass. A split second later Jonah's back thumped into the lawn below. The impact knocked all the air out of him and left him staring at stars. He fought for air until the stars retreated back into the sky and he sat up.

"Jonah? Are you okay?" Megan called.

He was about to say he was fine—no thanks to her—then changed his mind and groaned. He heard Megan catch her breath and he groaned again, louder this time.

"Don't move! I'm coming down," she said and disappeared inside.

Megan reappeared at the door in a white robe and slippers, her red hair tied back behind her head with a ribbon.

"I'll be all right," Jonah said breathlessly. "A bit winded. Maybe if I could sit down—get my breath back. Ouch! My ankle."

Megan glanced nervously at the upper windows of the house as if she expected to see her father glaring down at her. "Well, okay," she said, "but only for a while, and you have to promise not to make any noise."

He promised and almost forgot to limp in his hurry to get through the door.

Inside, Jonah perched on a wooden chair by the fishtank in the sitting room and watched Mr. Doherty's brightly colored fish swimming around the sunken castle while Megan went to fetch him a glass of water.

He had always liked the fish in that tank. He watched the Angelfish and the Black Lyretail Mollys. Leaning closer, he sent a group of Golden Barb, thin as gilded pins, darting away through the bubbles streaming from the aerator in the corner.

Megan returned with a glass of water.

"I'm sorry I knocked you off the window ledge," she said, "but you can't stay here long."

"I had to come, Meg."

She frowned. "Are you in some kind of trouble Jonah?"

He shrugged.

"You could at least tell me why you woke me up in the middle of the night, Jonah!"

"Because," he said, paused and thought, then went on, "you're the only friend I've got."

"Oh, I'm a friend again now, am I?"

"You always have been."

"I wouldn't be so sure. Maybe I've changed my mind."

"If you had, you wouldn't have sent Billy to warn me about Mr. Morran."

Megan looked as if she was going to say something but changed her mind and turned away.

"Look, Meg," Jonah said, "I'm sorry for all the things I've said and done. I didn't mean it. It just all sort of came out."

Megan shook her head. "I'm tired of trying to understand you, Jonah."

"Please, Meg—I need your help."

The word weighed heavy on the silence that followed. Megan looked at him as if puzzling over something very complicated, then her face softened slightly. "What have you done now, Jonah Ebbers?"

"Nothing. I just need a place to stay tonight."

"Well, you can't stay here!"

"I've got nowhere else to go."

She studied his face. "It's your father, isn't it?"

Jonah turned away. "Maybe," he said, watching the fish.

She stood for a while as if trying to make up her mind, then decided. He could sleep on the sofa, she said, as long as he was quiet and left all the talking to her in the morning.

Jonah swore he wouldn't cause any trouble and she crept upstairs to find him a blanket. While he waited, he watched the fish swimming in the tank. The gentle hum of the aerator and fizz of the bubbles had a soothing effect on him. He gazed at the fish finning through the water, but as he stared, the water seemed to deepen. The colors began to change, turning aquamarine at the surface, but darkening the deeper he looked, as if somehow he was staring into the depths of a great ocean. In the deep, a monster stirred.

He watched as the sleek shape turned slowly. Easily. Gracefully. Moving with a barely visible sweep of its tail. Its belly was gray; its back, sandy brown and striped black. It was a monster of the deep, blunt-nosed and solid, the dorsal fin on the ridge of its back cutting through the water without a trace. The tiger shark was hunting.

"What's wrong?" Megan asked, as she came down the stairs carrying a pillow and blanket.

"Look, Meg! Look!" he said, pointing. "Can't you see it?"

Megan came to stand beside him and peered into the fishtank. "See what?"

"The shark, of course!"

"Don't be so stupid."

He turned on her, wild-eyed. "It's right there! You must be able to see it!"

"You're scaring me, Jonah."

He was scaring himself.

Jonah watched in horror as the shark started rising, arrowing up from the deep with steady, rhythmical beats of its tail.

"It's attacking!" he gasped. "Look out, Meg! Look out!"

He was shouting. Screaming at her. He pushed her out of the way as the great fish came up. He was vaguely aware of lights coming on upstairs. He could hear Megan's father. Billy's voice too. There was confusion. Footsteps on the landing and stairs. But Jonah's mind was gripped by terror of the shark.

It opened its jaws and he saw the rows of jagged teeth, sharp as needles and razor edged.

"Get away from me!" he screamed.

He saw the shark's gills flaring on the sides of his great head as they pumped water. He saw the dead look in its eye as it fixed on him.

Suddenly the wooden chair was in his hands. Lunging, he desperately tried to fend off the attack. Somewhere, someone was shouting, "Stop him! He's having a fit." But it was too late. As the shark closed in, Jonah hurled the chair into its gaping jaws.

The glass of the fishtank shattered with the impact, releasing a wave of water that bulged out and flooded onto the floor. It was all over in a matter of seconds, the water spreading wide to leave a trail of colored fish flapping on the carpet, drowning in air.

Jonah stood staring into the void where the fishtank had been. The shark had vanished.

"Told you he was totally psycho," Billy whispered.

Jonah stood amid the junk in the garage at White Bird Cottage and leaned over his surfboard. It bridged the gap between the workbench and a broken chair. He was wearing his wetsuit.

He closed his eyes and caressed the board, running his fingers along the curve of the rocker and back down the rails. He picked up the ball of surf wax and began working it into the deck near the tail of the board. The wax was as yellow as butter and tacky to the touch, and would give his feet better grip when he was slashing white water.

"Jonah?"

One of the big doors lurched and scraped outward. Megan stood with an aura of brightness around her, the watery sunlight catching on the motes of dust suspended in the air. He stopped what he was doing. Stared at her. Then went back to waxing without a word.

"Jonah—we have to talk."

"What about?"

"You know perfectly well what."

"Look, I told your father I'll pay for the tank and the fish," he said, without pausing from his labors. "I've got money saved. I'll pay him back— all of it."

"I don't care about the money."

"Then why are you here?" Jonah looked at her.

"I thought you said you never wanted to see me again as long as you lived."

A long pause.

"I did say that," she admitted, "but I was angry. Scared. Oh, I don't know—it all happened so fast!" She took a step toward him. "But I've had time to think now. That's why I've come. I wanted to tell you I was wrong—that I'm sorry."

"Listen—" Jonah started.

"No, you listen," she interrupted. "I was awake all night thinking about what happened and I've come to tell you that I believe you."

"You're just saying that."

"No, I mean it."

"Why?"

"Because of what I saw—the look on your face. The fear. It was in your eyes, Jonah. No one could fake something like that. No one!" she said. "Don't get me wrong, I can't explain it. I don't know why it happened, or how, but I believe you really did see something terrible. That's why you broke the fishtank. Not because you're crazy in the head or were having a fit like the others say, but because you truly believed what you saw. And you were trying to protect me from it."

She returned his gaze steadily until he looked down, flicking at some small blemish on his board with a fingernail chewed to the quick.

"What's happening to me, Meg?" he asked after a long pause.

"I don't know, Jonah. I wish I did, but I don't."

Jonah shook his head sadly as if he had already decided something. "Billy's right. Your father's right. Everyone's right. I'm bad news, Meg. You have to stay away from me!"

He dropped the wax in with the other junk on the workbench and picked up his board.

"Where are you going?"

"Skullcrack. I don't care who sees me. I need waves."

She caught his arm as he pushed past. "Just promise me you won't go and hurt yourself again, Jonah," she said. "At least promise me that!"

He looked deep into her green eyes and suddenly found himself wondering what it would be like to kiss her. For a moment, he imagined himself doing it. Right there, in the garage, surrounded by the junk of his life. He felt the heat in his face. "Go home, Meg," he said, breaking away quickly.

*

As desperate for the ocean as he was, Jonah resisted the temptation to go to Craxkull Point via Gallagher's gate. Instead, he turned down the hill toward Mulligan, trotting along the lane until he reached a gap in the hedge that marked the start of the public footpath that ran along the cliffs. He could approach Craxkull Point under the cover of the shrubs and red heather that grew in thick clumps all the way there from Gorag's Hurl.

He followed the path as it twisted along the edges of the fields with the long drop to the sea on his right, until he reached the hedge at the bottom corner of Gallagher's field. From there he could see the surfers' tents through the twigs and branches. The van was parked alongside, near the gate into the lane. He could hear Eddie and the others talking, but could only make out snippets of what they were saying about surfing farther up the coast. Woodsmoke drifted away toward Craxkull Point and there was a delicious smell of sausages sizzling in their own juices.

Ahead lay open ground. The path was exposed where the shrubbery had been beaten flat and ravaged by the wind. He guessed it was a gap of about 50 yards and realized they would catch up with him easily if they noticed him before he reached the bushes near Craxkull Point.

Here goes, he thought, tucking his board tight up under his arm. He took a deep breath, climbed through the gap in the hedge, and ran.

Brown Cat spotted him first. Jonah heard him shout to the others: "Look! It's that kid!"

Out of the corner of his eye Jonah saw Eddie jump to his feet. Macca was pointing. "And he's got a stick with him."

"Told you he was lying!" Eddie snarled and grabbed his board. The sausages were knocked into the fire and forgotten in the rush.

The sound of feet thumping into the path behind him drove Jonah on. He was over halfway there but Eddie and the others were closing on him fast. The bushes approached, but agonizingly slowly. They seemed to hang back deliberately, then, after what seemed like an age, leapt up around him in sudden thorny bursts. He ducked low, running doubled up until he slipped neatly into a near invisible gap in the heather. The undergrowth swallowed him as he slid to a stop, covering the paleness of his board with his body as he fought his heaving lungs in an effort to not breathe too loudly.

The sound of footsteps grew steadily louder, then thumped past. He heard Eddie cursing and swearing. The shouts began to fade. Jonah slithered farther under the bushes, paused, then wormed his way to the hidden path. He was well out of sight by the time he heard the sound of voices returning.

"I'll get you, kid!" Eddie's fury echoed around the black rocks.

Jonah smiled.

Skullcrack greeted him like a long lost friend, calling to him in the boom and crash of the surf. Jonah answered the call. He zipped up his wetsuit and threw himself, body and soul, into the water's rush.

The waves pummeled him playfully as he paddled out lying flat on his board. A slow crawl. The cold gripping his head. Sometimes ducking through the walls of water, sometimes letting himself be carried up the face to hang in the air on the crest before swooping down the back in a rush. His strokes were easy. Relaxed. But he was buzzing inside as he made it out beyond the break.

He sat up on his board and greeted Skullcrack with a pinky and thumb salute. The waves lifted and rolled under him. He let the boom-crash beat fill his head and he sucked the air deep into his lungs, tasting the salt on his lips. Instantly, he felt himself coming back from that faraway place that lay somewhere deep inside himself. That gray, colorless place into which he had withdrawn. A place where only wraiths and shadows existed. A dead place.

He watched as a wave came at him like a heavy weight. Jonah took it on. He charged with it, timing the jump perfectly and making an easy turn. The wave curled in with a right hook and he ducked inside, thumped back off the lip and cut an angled gash down its face. He broke cleanly, laughing as the wave fell with a crash.

"Knockout!" The exhilaration whooped out of him as he punched the air.

High on the cliffs above, he saw three figures standing in sharp relief against the sky. Eddie, Macca, and Brown Cat had stopped searching for the way down and were watching him. They stood in a line with their surfboards at their sides like pointed shields. After a while, one by one, they turned and slipped off the skyline.

Skullcrack was his again. And for a short while, life seemed sweet.

*

The day was fading, hovering on the edge of night in that strange twilight pause that softens and smudges the sharpness of the world and foretells the chill of the coming darkness.

Jonah had left Skullcrack very late, surfing for as long as he dared, then feeling his way up the hidden path until he reached the top. Now he lay in the bushes. Watching. Waiting. Fearing a trap.

It soon became apparent that he needn't have worried. He could see the lights of the van, but

Eddie and the others seemed too busy to notice him. Brown Cat was standing on the roof, loading the things Eddie and Macca tossed up to him. As the flat shapes of their boards were being passed up and stowed, Jonah was easing himself out from under the shrubbery and creeping back along the cliffs the way he had come.

It was dark by the time Jonah reached home. The house was cold and empty, his father's motorcycle missing. Inside, it seemed strangely quiet—even the demons of White Bird Cottage were silent—and it felt hollow. He lit the fire, but the chill remained.

He looked out of the window when he heard the sound of an engine in the lane. Lights slid through the darkness as someone drove down the hill toward Mulligan. "You'll never catch me," he said, pulling the ragged curtains.

He went into the kitchen in search of something to eat and was lucky. He found some bread and enough jam to spread thinly on it. He folded the slices carelessly in half and stuffed them into his mouth. As he chewed, he noticed that his flannel "fish" and the stone "eggs" were lying on the floor and frowned. Then Jonah saw the cap.

It was lying in the rubbish as if it had been hurled into the corner. Jonah picked it up. It reminded him of Mr. Morran's. Puzzled, he looked around and started noticing other things amid all the usual mess.

The more he looked, the more he saw signs that a fight had taken place in the kitchen, until finally he saw the remains of the bottle smashed against the wall. Suddenly, the demons of White Bird Cottage were back, whispering about his father again:

Sssssame Old Agony.

*

The dresser in Jonah's room had been ransacked. The drawer wrenched out, emptied, and the contents trampled. The tin lay on the floor among the clothes. Its lid was missing. His precious things had been spilled and scattered.

The money was gone, of course, but worse—much worse—the photographs of his mother had been torn in half, then half again, and the pieces scattered like ashes. He felt numb as he hunted for them, his hands shaking as he tried to fit her face back together again. He traced her torn smile with his fingers. The tears burned the backs of his eyes and he rubbed furiously at his face.

"Why did you have to go and do that, Dad? Why?" Suddenly the numbness turned to rage.

It started deep in the pit of his stomach and boiled up inside him like magna. Boiling, blinding rage erupted from him in a snarl. He hurled himself around the walls, kicking and punching without caring as he slammed into the stone. Round and round he went, in a dizzying, violent whirl. Then, as quickly as it had come upon him, the rage left him and he felt cold inside.

"I've got to get away from this stinking place!"

He found his clothes and changed quickly, rolling his wetsuit up and stuffing it into an overnight bag. He knew it wasn't going to be easy. He had no money, no transportation and no place to go. He didn't care. He packed the few clothes worth taking, remembered his toothbrush, and took the clock from his bedside table. It was while he was picking up the last pieces of the photographs that he had an idea.

It was so simple he wondered why he hadn't thought of it straight away. "I'll tell them how to get down to Skullcrack." He spoke it aloud. "I'll tell them in exchange for a lift. I'll make them take me as far away from here as possible."

And despite every instinct telling him not to go with Eddie and the others, Jonah knew he had no choice.

The bag thumped onto the floor as he dropped it through the trapdoor into the living room below. He climbed down the ladder after it and took one last look around, noticing the book of poetry lying where he had left it. With one quick movement, he scooped it up and stuffed it into his bag, then headed out the back way to pick up his surfboard. He wrote, "I am out of here. I won't be coming back," on a piece of paper that he propped up on the kitchen table. He was about to leave when his father came staggering in through the back door.

Wex Ebbers leaned heavily against the door frame, his face flushed with the spirit that heated his belly. He squinted at the overnight bag in Jonah's hand. "And what's going on here?"

"Where's my money?" Jonah snapped.

"Your money? And there was me thinking it was just a small part of what you owed me for all the years I've looked after you. For feeding and clothing you. For looking after you!" He sneered. "Well, it isn't your money any longer. It's Big Bernard's. He's got it all now." He grinned. "And my credit's good again down at The Finger."

"You make me sick," Jonah said, turning away.

His father caught hold of his arm. "And where do you think you're going?"

"As far away from here as possible."

"Away? Just like that? After all I've done for you!"

"I'm sick of your drinking and lying."

"Now you're beginning to sound like that Mr. Morran," his father growled. "Coming 'round here, telling me how to run my life. Said I wasn't treating you right! Said he'd even written a letter warning me. Well, I showed that liar! I taught the teacher a lesson."

"Take your thieving hands off me, Dad!"

"So it's Master High and Mighty Jonah Ebbers, is it? Well, I'm not the only one who takes things around here. You've been sticking your nose in where it's not wanted! Snooping in my private stuff. Stealing my photographs!"

Jonah glared at him. "You shouldn't have done that to them, Dad."

His father glowered back. He made a noise in his throat and pushed Jonah away. "Go on then! Go! You won't last a minute out there. You'll come crawling back again soon enough."

"That's where you're wrong," Jonah said. "I've got friends with a van and they're going to give me a ride as far away from you as possible."

"You! Friends! Don't make me laugh."

"That's good coming from you, Dad." Jonah pushed past him and out through the back door.

"I warn you," his father said, following him, "if you walk out on me now I'll never have you back. Never! I swear it. I'll never see you again as long as I live—just like I'll never see that damn sister of yours, no matter how many letters she writes!"

Jonah stared. "What did you say?"

"Nothing! Forget it!"

"You said my sister?"

His father staggered back into the kitchen.

Jonah went after him.

His father was leaning heavily on the kitchen table, his shoulders hunched, his head bowed low. "I've said it now," he muttered, "he may as well know the whole truth." He turned to Jonah. "You've got a sister. A twin sister. She's called Sally Marie. There! Now you know. I've been keeping that secret for too long."

His words stole Jonah's breath and set Jonah's blood pumping, hot in his face and head. "A sister," he said, his breath coming back in a rush. Then his head filled with broken thoughts and he grabbed his father by the collar and shook him. "I've had a sister all my life and you never even told me!"

"I have now." His father shook him off easily and pushed him back through the open door. "So just go if you're going!" he snarled. He saw the surfboard leaning against the wall and picked it up. "And take this piece of junk with you!"

As he held out the board, a sudden change came over him. It was as if all the disappointment and futility of his life seemed to overcome him, focusing all of his hurt and hatred on the surfboard.

Jonah saw the look on his father's face. "No! Dad," he pleaded. "Please don't!"

Too late.

With one swift movement, his father lifted the board high over his head, stood for a moment like an executioner with an ax ready to fall, then brought the board down into the ground with all his might. He ground the nose into the earth, mangling the rigid plastic so that it splintered and popped and broke into three pieces.

His father began to change before Jonah's eyes. The man seemed to grow, suddenly becoming huge and hunched. Terrifying. His eyes disappearing into mean little slits. His mouth and nose bulging into a snout. Slowly, inexorably he morphed into a monstrous pig-beast, belching on a bellyful of black beer and spirits.

A snarl peeled back the beast's lips. It broke from its mouth in a bellowing roar, so loud the sound seemed to grip Jonah's head and crush his brain. Then the beast came at him with a gurgling rush.

His fist punched out of the darkness incredibly fast. Instinctively Jonah ducked, but he heard a dull smack as it caught him on the cheek.

The impact knocked him back, spinning him around in a whirl of arms and legs. Twisted, he fell to the ground—hard. He lay there, dazed and numb, until the hurt stabbed through his cheek and jabbed into his brain.

Jonah cried out as the beast loomed over him. But even as he pleaded with it, the monster was already changing shape again. Shrinking. Its hideous snout melting away and its eyes growing wide with horror and disbelief.

"What have I done?" his father gasped.

"Stay away from me!" Jonah scrambled back through the mud. He found his feet and ran.

"Wait! Jonah! Come back! I didn't mean to!" The shouts followed him but he shut his ears to them and ran on blindly into the darkness.

The branches of the old oak creaked as he blundered through the shadows until he reached Gallagher's gate. It was open. The field was silent and empty in the moonlight. The van, the tents, Eddie, Macca, and Brown Cat had all gone.

"No! Come back! Please! I'll tell you how to get down to Skullcrack!" Jonah was screaming at the top of his voice as he ran about wildly. Sobbing, his breath came in ragged gasps. His feet slipped and slid, tangling in the long grass, until a great nothingness opened before him. Suddenly, the sea was stretched out wide and flat at his feet.

The water shimmered in the distance where the moonlight touched it. And far below, in the velvet blackness at the foot of the cliff, he heard the boom of the surf, calling him.

Without warning, the ragged edge crumbled away in a cascade of loose earth and stones and sent him slithering down into the darkness. Down in a sudden terrifying rush. Down, without hope of saving himself. Down, until he felt the wind on his face, and then...nothing.

Jonah murmured and stirred. He was dreaming of the white birds. They were flying in circles high above, the soft beat of their wings mingling with the scratch of their cries.

In his dream, he was lying on a narrow ledge on the side of a sheer cliff. He felt deathly cold. The first rays of the sun caught on the black rocks and set them alight: cold heat, blood red. Below, a wave surged up and crashed. The next came higher and the next higher still, until finally he felt icy tongues of spray lick his face.

He gasped and opened his eyes. He lay in bed, blinking at the fluorescent light on the ceiling above him, listening to an unfamiliar beeping noise. After a while he sat up, shivering despite the heat of the room.

"How did I get here?" He looked around, trying to remember, but couldn't.

He was wearing white pajamas. The room was bare and clinical. It had a window, a door, a bed, and a single plastic chair. He knew at once that it was a hospital room.

He pulled back the sheets, stood up and was just about to open the door when his father was ushered into the room by a nurse. His father's face was ashen. His hair disheveled. His chin covered by thick stubble.

"Dad! What's happened? What am I doing in the hospital?"

His father looked straight through him as if he were invisible. The big man hung back from the bed, then eventually sank heavily onto the plastic chair at the bedside. "What have I done to you, Jo?" he said in a hoarse whisper.

Only then did Jonah look at the bed again. He frowned. Somehow, someone had slipped into it without him noticing. Someone about his age with a bandage around his head. A respirator pipe snaked to a mask over the boy's nose and mouth, a drip led to the needle in his arm and wires to pads on his chest. The monitor above the bed announced every beat of his heart with a steady electronic peep, peep, peep.

"But I'm here now, Jo," he heard his father say.

Jonah frowned. "Dad! Can't you see me? Can't you...." The words died on his lips. He looked again at the boy on the bed. He saw the bruise on his cheek and the dark hair beneath the bandage. "No!" He shook his head. "No, it can't be!"

But it was. It was his own bruised and battered body lying in that hospital bed. And suddenly he began remembering.

"The doctor said I should keep talking to you, Jo," Jonah heard his father say. "She said you can probably hear me even though you're in a coma."

"A coma!" The word sent a shiver through him. "But I can't be. I'm standing here."

He looked around. The walls seemed less solid, as if they were made out of mist—mist lit by a strange light.

As soon as Jonah had noticed the light, he found he could think of nothing else. He had an overwhelming urge to see where it was coming from but as he turned to look, he found something was holding him back. His hand was being squeezed as if it were being gripped. He looked back at the bed and saw his father had reached out and was holding his hand.

"If you can hear me, Jo," his father said, "I want you to know I never meant to hurt you. It all just got out of control. You have to believe that." There was a long pause, then, "When I found out you'd fallen from Craxkull Point I thought...." His voice cracked and he left the rest unsaid. He recovered and tried to sound more cheerful. "You were lucky, though. If you hadn't landed on that ledge there wouldn't have been much the rescue fellas could have done. It was a grand rescue—with a helicopter and everything. You should've seen it, Jo."

His father's voice trailed away and he was silent for a while. The quiet was disturbed only by the constant peep, peep, peep of the monitor.

Jonah remembered the light and saw that it had begun to fade. He noticed that it grew brighter when he looked at it. He felt the urge to go to it. Then he heard his father's voice again:

"I've never talked about your mother much."

Jonah paused, listening. The light began to fade again.

"I loved her, despite what you might think," his father said, pulling out the two torn photographs. Jonah could see they had been stuck back together with tape. His father smiled. "We had happy times. White Bird Cottage was our first home. She named it after her favorite poem by W. B. Yeats." The smile faded. "You weren't even a year old when she died in that crash. It was terrible. I didn't think I could go on living." He paused. "But there was you and your sister to look after, so I had to for your sakes."

He took a deep breath before he went on. "I tried to be a good father. I thought I could cope. I can see now I was wrong." He gripped Jonah's hand tighter. "I'm not making excuses for what I've done. God knows, it wasn't easy giving your sister up. It still hurts..." a long pause, then he sighed and added, "except when I drink."

He closed his eyes and bowed his head. "I kept thinking I could manage a boy. But a girl! What did I know about looking after a girl? I told myself a girl needs a mother. Then I heard about an adoption agency in Dublin. They offered to help make her life better than I ever could hope to."

Another long pause.

"Your mother chose the name Sally," his father said. "I called her Sally Marie in memory of her. It seemed right."

The tears were running down his face and it made Jonah wince to see him cry. "Why didn't you tell me all this before?" he said. "Why, Dad?"

His father answered as if he had heard him. "I wanted to tell you. A hundred times. But I just couldn't. I was afraid of what you'd think of me. I was afraid you'd hate me and the thought of losing the one good thing I had left in my life was too much. So I kept telling myself, what's past is past and the future would be different, better. Guess I was wrong about that too."

He let go of Jonah's hand, stood up and began pacing the floor. "Soon after we buried your mother, the adoption agency called and said they had found Sally a home with an American couple, an engineer and his wife who were moving back to Florida to live." He ceased his pacing.

"I had to let her go, don't you see? It was for the best. They had money. They could give her everything." He sat down heavily, slumping back onto the chair, and stared at the floor miserably. "I tried not to think of her. I tried to forget. But I couldn't. That's why I started going to The Crooked Finger."

He shook his head. "I heard nothing for years, then about a year ago the letters started arriving. The adoption agency forwarded them."

He reached into the pocket of his jacket and pulled out a small bundle. He smoothed the letters flat on the bed. Jonah recognized them as the ones he had seen in the wooden chest.

"When I saw her name on the back, all the bad memories came flooding back. I got angry. I thought they had no right to go telling her about me. I told myself it was all wrong to drag up the past after all these years. That's why I decided not to read them. That's why I swore I would burn them," he said. He sighed again. "But I just couldn't do it. I just couldn't. So I locked them away in that chest, along with everything else that made me think."

He leaned close to Jonah. "The truth is, Jo," he whispered, "I was scared of what the letters might mean for me—for us." He glanced down at them. "I was scared to write back and tell her the truth. That her father is a drunk who works in a stinking fish cannery all day."

His father's head fell onto the crisp white sheet. In the long silence that followed, Jonah realized his father was no longer holding his hand. Jonah turned toward the light. Free to go, he walked over to the wall and looked though the mistiness. Beyond it, everything was hazy and indistinct. Only the light seemed to exist and out of it seemed to radiate a feeling of great peacefulness. Somehow he knew his mother was out there somewhere, beyond those four walls of that hospital room. Waiting.

The room, shrouded in white, seemed cold in comparison. Jonah looked back into the warm light.

"It's time I made up for what I've done, Jo," he heard his father say. "It'll be all right. If only you'll come back to me. If only you'll wake up."

Jonah found himself thinking of the sister he had never met. He thought of his father and of White Bird Cottage, of Fergus and the Sligo Queen, of the way the surf peeled on Skullcrack, and of the dolphins. He thought of Megan when she smiled. Then he thought of his sister again. Instantly, Jonah knew he wasn't ready.

The mist began to stir around him. Shreds of it tore away from the walls and were sucked toward the bed. It was as if a giant plug had been pulled and suddenly everything was being drawn down. The vortex grew in strength. The wind buffeted him. He stumbled. The tremendous rush of air dragged on him, sucking him across the room until he reached the bed and fell onto his own body. He felt himself sinking into it, melting as he became one with his body once more.

A moment later, he opened his eyes and blinked at his father at his bedside.

"Dad?" he croaked, "Dad, is that you?"

*

Megan looked up as she finished reading. "This is so weird—your sister sounds just like you!"

Jonah nodded. "And you should see the other letters, Meg. They're full of questions about a brother, but there's no way she could have known about me. Dad told the adoption agency Sal was his only child."

"That is weird."

Jonah nodded.

They weren't identical twins, of course, and according to his father Sal was the older by three minutes or so. Jonah wished she had sent a photograph of herself. The only one he had was the photograph he had found in the wooden chest. She turned out to be the baby in red.

While Jonah had been recovering from his fall he had spent a lot of time thinking about her, how she would look now. How she would sound. And he had come to a conclusion.

He turned to Megan. "Do you think there could be a sort of bond between a brother and a sister, even though neither knew the other one existed?"

Megan thought about it. "I saw this documentary once. It was about these twins who'd been separated when they were very young. Neither knew about the other, but when they finally met, years later, they found they liked exactly the same things. They wore the same type of clothes. Drove the same sort of cars. They even had the same breed of dogs—terriers, I think it was."

"Lots of people have terriers," Jonah said.

"Not both called Siegfried!"

Jonah had to admit that was unusual.

"And look," Megan said, pointing to the letter, "she even likes surfing!"

More than three weeks had passed since he had been discharged from the hospital. They were in the library at the end of Jonah's first full day back at school. He had told no one, not even Megan, exactly what had driven him to Craxkull Point that night. Nor had he spoken of the strange light he had seen while he was in hospital. Only the scar on his forehead served as an outward reminder of his fall, and, like the hurt, the memory of that terrible night had begun to fade as calm had settled over White Bird Cottage.

Jonah stopped writing, tore the page off the pad, and crumpled it up. He tossed it in the bin with the eleven other attempts he had made at writing the letter during library period. He looked at Megan. "You're not helping me much."

He had made up his mind to write to Sal, but he didn't know how to begin. The words burned inside him, but they looked all wrong when he wrote them down. They needed to be spoken.

The bell rang. Jonah and Megan gathered up their books and joined the rush for the door. Billy was waiting for Megan in the hall.

"You could be right," Megan said, walking. "Having a twin sister could explain everything."

"Like what?"

"Like why you keep seeing things, for a start. It's probably the power of the mind. E.S.P. You know, telepathy or something."

Jonah thought about what Megan had said. Secretly, he had already come to the same conclusion. In one of her letters, Sal had described Storm Island: the house on the beach, the palm trees around Green Turtle Bay, the way the white sand curved to a lighthouse on a rocky point.

He had recognized the description immediately. He had seen that place before. The Bone Man had taken him there in a sort of weird, living dream. All of which had made him wonder about the girl he had seen there, and if, by some strange twist of fate, he might not already have seen his long lost sister without even knowing it.

However, a part of his brain still denied it. The part that told him things like that weren't possible. The same part that tried to ignore the warning of the Bone Man.

"A word with you, Jonah," Mr. Morran said, catching up with them in the hall. He drew Jonah to one side. "Your father came to see me yesterday. He apologized for losing control when I called, and he said he's quit drinking. I'm glad to hear it, for your sake. We have to make sure he sticks to that promise. I'll be keeping an eye on him, but you're going to have to help, Jonah. Promise you'll tell me next time if things get bad. You can't go on covering up for him."

Jonah shrugged.

"I'm not asking you to spy on him, Jonah. Just to help him."

"Okay."

"That's good. The principal has asked me to drop in again tonight to see how you're doing."

"Tonight!" Jonah was startled.

Mr. Morran nodded. "I'll be over as soon as I finish here." He walked away, then turned. "Oh and by the way, next time you accidentally forget to deliver one of my notes I'll boil up one of those flannel fish of yours and watch while you eat it!"

The ride home seemed to take forever—thanks mainly to Gallagher's cows blocking the lane—but eventually the bus pulled in under the old oak and Jonah burst through the doors as they hissed open. He didn't stop until he got home.

His father's motorcycle wasn't there.

"Oh no! Not again! Not tonight!" Jonah gasped, his heart turning to lead as he opened the door.

He stopped and looked around. The kitchen was tidy. The sink empty. The floor clean. He could even smell something cooking in the oven.

His father was sitting by the fire in the living room, waiting for him. His hair was combed and slicked back. His face was cleanly shaven and he was even wearing a clean shirt. But Jonah could still see that the same jaundiced look was in his eye and he noticed the way his father's hands trembled slightly as they rested on his big knees.

"I've been waiting for you, Jo," he said. "I want to talk to you about something, something important." He waited for Jonah to sit down before he continued. "As you know, I haven't touched a drop of alcohol since that night. And I've sworn I never will again. But I have to be honest, Jo. It won't be easy, even the doctors say that."

"I'll help you, Dad."

His father smiled. "You're a good lad, Jo, but it isn't quite as simple as that. I've been drinking so long the Old Agony has got into my blood," he said. "It's like a worm inside my head that I'll never get rid of. I'm afraid it'll eat away at me until I give into it again."

"You can beat it, Dad. I know you can."

He shook his head. "I can't risk it. I don't want what happened to ever happen again. I need to know you're safe. That's why I talked with the adoption agency—"

"No!" Jonah was on his feet. "I won't let you send me away too!"

His father held up his hands. "You know I'd never do that, Jo."

"But you said—"

"Let me explain," his father interrupted. "There's something I've got to do if I'm to have a hope of beating this thing. It won't be easy. But I've made up my mind." He paused. "I have to face up to the past, Jo, or there'll be no future."

Jonah stared at him. "What do you mean?"

"I've decided it's time to make amends for what I've done, Jo. That's why I called the agency, to get the telephone number of your sister's new..."

he swallowed hard as if the words stuck in his throat, "...parents, Connie and Dan Dayton."

"You've talked to Sal!"

He shook his head. "I tried to call from the phone in The Crooked Finger, but I couldn't get any answer," he said. "But I went ahead all the same and I did it."

"What? What did you do, Dad?"

"I bought two tickets to the United States."

"Don't make me laugh!"

"No joke," his father said. "I'm taking a week off work and I've spoken to your principal. He says it's okay for you to miss a few days, considering the circumstances." He stood up as if they were going to leave that moment.

"So there's nothing to stop us, Jo. The tickets are paid for and I've arranged for our passports with the immigration office in Dublin."

"But tickets to America cost a bundle," Jonah said. "Where did you find that sort of money?" He gasped. "You sold your bike!"

"It's done," his father said firmly. "The bike wasn't important and I made enough to pay for the tickets and the hotels, if they're not too expensive. We're going, Jo. Nothing is going to stop us. Nothing."

"I've kept you two apart for too long. I want to make up for that. I want you to meet your sister and try to make up for some of that lost time. And I hope maybe you'll both find it in your hearts to forgive me for what I've done, Jo. Then maybe we can start all over again and be happy."

The United States National Environmental Satellite Service picked it up first and flashed a warning to the computer screens of weather stations from Florida, as far west as Texas and as far north as North Carolina: *10° N. 45° W. Tropical Storm. Building. Expect Hurricane Force. Imminent.*

To the west of the scattered Windward Islands, about a thousand miles from the Venezuelan coast of South America, the pressure was dropping fast over the tropical waters of the Western Atlantic. Late in the hurricane season, one of the most awesome and deadly cycles of nature had been set in motion.

Warm, saturated air was rising, sucked up by winds high in the troposphere. As the air rose, it grew even warmer. As it grew warmer, it rose faster and dragged in more moisture-laden air behind it at sea level.

As the rising air touched the cooler air high above it, it condensed in towering cumulus clouds. They heaped up one on another like giant water balloons that split and burst open to release a deluge of rain that, in turn, fueled the cycle: more rain, more moisture, more latent heat, more sultry air rising, sucking in more air behind it in a rush of wind as the clouds built up higher and more torrential rain fell. This was the birth of a storm.

It took all the awesome power of the planet itself to set the storm in motion. The rotation of the Earth on its axis set the clouds spinning as the Coriolis forces took effect. The giant thunderheads were drawn tight to form a spiral of tremendous size around a clear blue center. At its head, the cirrus clouds were thrown outward in a wispy spin. At its base, the winds spiraled inward with increasing speed and the rain blasted down.

From its cradle in the Atlantic, the hurricane tracked in a northwesterly direction and got lost for a while in the vast expanse of the ocean, but all the while it was growing. Gorging itself. Feeding its terrible power. Soon, it was more than two hundred miles in diameter and growing.

It accelerated as it approached the Windward Islands, then veered north sharply. By the time it slammed into the Leeward Islands of Dominica and Guadeloupe, with wind speeds of more than 125 miles an hour, the storm had been given the highest rating on the hurricane scale and it had been given a name: Hurricane Edwin.

*

The flight to Orlando took nearly ten hours. First, they had flown from Dublin to London on Aer Lingus and connected with their scheduled American Airlines 747 which, with the five-hour time difference, landed on time at Orlando International Airport just after 4 P.M.

As they collected their small bags from the baggage carousel, they had no way of knowing they had flown into the path of one of the biggest storms on record.

Jonah had tried not to let his sense of foreboding overshadow the excitement of his first flight, but it hadn't been easy. His every instinct warned him of the shadow that was creeping closer. Had he known what it was, or that satellites high above the earth were tracking its course too—he would have trembled at its awesome power. But neither he, nor anyone else, knew just how devastating that hurricane would be.

The heat hit Jonah and his dad as they walked out of the air-conditioned terminal building. It seemed to press down on them, as heavy and sweaty as a Sumo wrestler. It sapped their energy, and by the time they had found a Greyhound bus to take them most of the way to Storm Island, their clothes were drenched with sweat.

"Is it always as hot as this here in October?" his father asked the man sitting across the aisle.

The man was thin and wizened, his face baked by the sun, but his teeth gleamed white as he grinned and turned to the big woman in the floral dress sitting beside him. "You hear that, Ma? This guy thinks it's hot."

"You just arrived?" asked the man. He introduced himself as, "Sam Cootill but everyone calls me Coot." He pushed up the brim of his filthy baseball cap with his thumb.

Wex Ebbers mopped his brow with a handkerchief and nodded.

Coot smiled. "Well, I'm telling you, it'll get a whole heap hotter yet before it storms some."

Coot and his wife lived in Bridgewater, the last town on the mainland before Storm Island, and he was a bit of an expert on the weather, especially storms. And while October was late in the season, it was still hot enough for hurricanes.

There was a saying around there, Coot told them, which went: "Too soon in June. Stand by in July. It could bust in August. Remember September. It should be all over by the end of October. But the late will always be great."

"They used to name hurricanes after women," he said, smiling as he shot a glance toward his wife as if she had been one of them. "But now they alternate names so there's equality. Hurricane Hugo was bad, but Andrew was worse. When it hit Florida, it took only three hours to make 160,000 people homeless." He whistled appreciatively. "But I reckon there's an even bigger storm still to come." He rubbed his knees through the cotton of his pale blue slacks. "I can feel it in my bones. Last time my joints creaked this bad, we were hit by Hurricane Georges."

"There you go again, talking up a storm," his wife said, clicking her tongue disapprovingly.

Coot laughed. "That's just plain superstition, Ma, and you know it. How can it make a straw of difference what I say?"

"It doesn't mostly," she said, "but I still reckon you should be careful what you say about hurricanes. They've got ears as well as an eye, that's for sure."

The bus had seen better days. A big silver coach with broken air conditioning and vinyl seats that stuck to the backs of Jonah's legs and made him sweat even more. Earl, the driver, knew Coot and his wife well. He'd run them up to Orlando a few days before to see the family. Big and friendly, Earl sat with his elbow resting out the open window as he maneuvered the rattling bus through the rush of Orlando's traffic.

Jonah watched the sprawling suburbs pass by, reading the signs for Disney, MGM, and Universal Studios and wondering if they would have enough money left to visit any of them. He doubted it. Eventually, the forest of signs began to peter out as they headed east. The road stretched ahead of them. They crossed Highway 95 and turned north in the shadow of the launch towers of the space center and followed the Canaveral National Seashore north.

"Do you know Storm Island?" Jonah asked Coot during a lull in the conversation.

"Sure do!" he said. "Me and Ma have lived in Bridgewater all our lives and you've got to go through there to get to Storm."

Storm, he told them, was one of the islands just north of Cape Canaveral, a seven-mile finger of sand connected to the mainland by a road on a concrete causeway. Most of the people who lived there made their living by fishing.

"Got a place to stay over there?" Coot asked.

"Not exactly," Jonah's father had admitted. "Suppose we'll just find a hotel."

Coot shook his head. "Not many of them on Storm. You're better off staying in Bridgewater," Coot said. He and Ma exchanged glances and she nodded. Coot turned back to Jonah's father. "If you're looking for a place to stay tonight, I know somewhere that makes the best clam chowder around, ain't that right, Ma?"

Ma clucked and fussed at the compliment. However, the offer was genuine. Wex Ebbers accepted the free bed and board gratefully. They would go to the island in the morning.

"I know you want to see Sal just as soon as you can, Jo," his father said, patting him on the shoulder, "but it's getting late. It'll be better to wait. I'll phone the Daytons first thing. That way at least it won't be so much of a shock when we turn up on the doorstep."

By the time they reached Bridgewater, the palm trees were wiping away the last of the sunset with their fronds. Jonah's first glimpse of the island was a sharp-edged silhouette against the pinks of the sky, lights twinkling across the water.

Later, after a dinner of chowder, Jonah lay on the camp bed in the back room of the house and let the fan cool his face. It was after midnight and it seemed to be getting hotter. Not a breath of wind stirred the curtains as they hung, ghostly and translucent in the moonlight. The air was sultry and still.

He picked up the book of poetry and fingered the cover without looking at it. Inside he had the taped-up photographs of his mother and one of Sal's letters. Jonah had brought the book and photographs to show Sal when they finally met.

Sal was close, so close he could feel her presence right in his bones. He couldn't explain it; he just knew it deep inside himself. As if somehow their souls had been magnetized at birth and some invisible force was relentlessly drawing them together. But now that the moment had almost arrived for them to meet, Jonah felt nervous. He wondered what they would say to each other. He wondered what to do.

"She probably won't even like me." His thoughts whirled around and around his head like the fan above his bed.

He listened to the crickets in the garden outside his window. He breathed the warm scents and listened to the distant sound of the ocean. He began to drift. His eyelids fluttered and closed. And in the calm before the storm, he slept.

*

The Unblinking Eye moved across the dark water. Cloaked in clouds shot through with flickering tongues of lightning fire, Hurricane Edwin had grown to monstrous size. More than four hundred miles in diameter, it seemed almost without end. As the first clouds were hurrying toward the Atlantic coast of Florida, the center of the storm—the eye—was still two hundred miles to the southeast over the islands of the Bahamas.

The storm sent out heralds to bear witness to its majesty: Lightning. Thunder. Wind. Rain. Like the four horsemen of the apocalypse, the storm's angels were awesome in their power and yet they were as nothing to the power that surrounded the Unblinking Eye. Unleashed, they screamed over the ocean. Dread captains of destruction, they came racing across the water, devouring the sky and venting their wrath on the islands and ships unfortunate enough to be in their way, until finally they approached the mainland of America. And most, but not all, trembled and made ready to flee before them.

"Jo! Wake up!"

Jonah was shaken awake shortly before 5 A.M. He opened his eyes to see his father leaning over him.

"Get your things together, Jo. We're leaving."

Jonah rubbed the sleep from his eyes. He could hear the wind whistling on the telephone wires and the knocking of a loose weatherboard on the side of the house. He sat up in bed. "What's happening, Dad? What's wrong?"

His father's face was pale in the dim light. "Coot's bones were right. There is a storm coming, Jo. A big one. The radio says it has turned toward us and could hit the coast any time. Coot reckons we should get away inland. Go back to Orlando while we have the chance."

"But we just got here!" Jonah said as he slipped out of bed and into his board shorts and a T-shirt. "What about Sal?"

"I tried to phone, but the lines to Storm Island are jammed. Anyway, Coot says they're already evacuating the island."

"But if they do that we might never find her!"

"I know, Jo, but there's not a lot we can do. They're giving out warnings every fifteen minutes on the radio. The storm changed direction suddenly, hit the Bahamas last night, and is heading right this way. They're calling it a hurricane."

"A hurricane?"

He nodded. "Hurricane Edwin."

His father went on talking, telling Jonah how everything would be all right and that Coot had said there would be buses to evacuate people to shelters further inland, but Jonah heard none of it. His thoughts had stopped dead at the name.

"Beware Edwin!" As the Bone Man's warning echoed back to him, his head filled with laser images of light and he saw himself standing in the circle of stones once more. He pictured the storm as he had seen it then: the rain lashing down, the purple-black clouds swirling, and bolts of fire stabbing down from the sky. With a cold, dead feeling in his guts, he knew the storm had come for him.

He remembered when he had stood on the shore at Craxkull Point and had offered himself to the waves. Hadn't he made a bargain then? Hadn't he called up the storm? It had come for him now. But what if he wasn't enough? What if it wanted his other half too?

"We have to warn her, Dad!" he blurted, interrupting his father's directions about packing up. "We can't just leave her."

"Don't worry, Jo, they've probably evacuated the island by now."

"No! You don't understand. She's still here. I know she is. I just know!"

"How can you, Jo?" his father said. He shook his head. "Anyway, I can't risk taking you over to the island. We'll just have to wait until this storm blows itself out and hope for the best."

Jonah tucked the book and the photographs into his bag, but he had second thoughts about Sal's letter. He folded it carefully and put it in his pocket, just in case. He went downstairs.

Coot and Ma were staying.

"We'll take our chances here," Coot said as he bolted the storm shutters across the windows. They had seen storms come and go and were resigned to them as an inevitable part of living by the sea. "Anyway," he added, "we're too old to go starting over again. If the house goes, reckon we might as well go with it."

Ma Cootill had made sandwiches for them and fussed over Jonah as Coot dispensed some last-minute advice:

"Remember," he warned, "if you do get caught in it, concrete buildings are the safest places to shelter. But stay away from the windows and don't go out, no matter what. If the wind drops suddenly, then you'll know the eye of the storm is passing over you. It won't last long. Once it has passed, the storm will hit again just as bad as before. A wind like that can blow straws through a sheet of corrugated iron so you don't have a cat's chance if you're outside."

They hurriedly said their goodbyes and wished each other luck. Jonah and his father promised to come back to see they were all right when it was over.

It was 6:27 A.M. The wind was rising in gusts. High in the sky, cirrus clouds had blotted out the sunlight and turned it hazy. Now, thicker gray clouds were hurrying up from the southeast and

123

there was a shadow on the rim of the world. An ominously dark shadow, like night creeping back before its time, spread across the horizon as far as the eye could see.

Everywhere Jonah looked, people were hurriedly packing up and preparing to leave. Windows were being boarded up and nailed shut. Anything that moved was tied down. Some people were even roping down the roofs of their houses in an attempt to prevent them from being ripped off by the wind. It looked as if the people of Bridgewater were preparing for war.

"I put this down to the good old Ebbers' luck," his father joked grimly, as they joined people waiting to be evacuated by bus. "Who knows what'll happen next." It started to rain in sudden squally bursts that soaked them. "Should've kept my mouth shut," he grumbled as they waited.

Jonah glanced down the main street toward Storm Island. From where he stood, he could see the bridge. It was low and straight, crouching over the water like a concrete centipede on stumpy legs. He could see some of the bigger waves were already breaking over the parapet, but the island did not look far away. It was agonizingly close.

A bus arrived and everyone who could crammed themselves onto it, taking with them suitcases and the selected pieces of their lives: dogs, cats, a parrot in a wire cage, a rolled-up rug, someone even had a hatstand. The line shuffled forward. The doors hissed shut and the bus pulled away.

They waited for the next one and the next after that. The people around them began to show signs of unease. They became restless. There were murmurings. Someone wondered whether it wasn't already too late to leave. Another agreed: "Reckon it'll be safer back home in the basement than out on the open road," he said, just loud enough to make them all feel uncomfortable.

Then, at last, it was their turn.

"Room for five more!" the bus driver said as he counted the people on. "Hurry, man—or that sucker Edwin'll be whipping our sorry butts all the way to Orlando!"

"Come on, Jo!" His father threw their bags in through the open door.

"But we can't just leave Sal, Dad!"

"We've been through that already, Jo," his father coaxed, trying to sound reasonable. "Now come on!" He climbed aboard and reached a hand back to pull him up.

Jonah glanced toward the bridge, then back at his father. "Sorry, Dad! I just can't!"

And as he said it, everything seemed to happen at once. A sudden gust of wind pulled a deluge from the sky. The crowd surged forward. The line stretched, then broke, and everyone started pushing, panicking as they tried to shove onto the bus.

But still Jonah hung back.

"Out of the way, kid!" a big man snarled, shouldering Jonah out of the way.

"Too many! We're full! Wait for the next bus!" The bus driver was trying to restore order and close the doors.

"Wait! Please! That's my son!" Jonah heard his father shouting above the din. His father was trying to fight his way off the bus, but the aisle and doorway were jammed solid with people determined to fight their way on. The driver panicked and pulled away, spilling an overflow of people back onto the pavement as the doors shut.

"Dad!" Jonah ran after it, but the bus accelerated. He stopped in the middle of the road and could only watch as it drove on. A horn blared. He jumped back out of the way of a passing car. By the time he looked back, the bus had already turned the corner out of sight.

"Don't worry, Dad—I'll be OK and I'll find her," he said. Then he turned and ran back down the street toward the bridge and the coming storm.

A whistle shrilled.

"Hey kid! Where do you think you're going?"

The police patrol stopped Jonah as he approached the bridge. Two police officers were standing beside their car, which was parked by the side of the bridge with its lights flashing. They were attempting to keep a constant stream of traffic moving off the bridge and up the main street of Bridgewater.

The one with the whistle beckoned to him with his baton. "I asked you a question."

"To Storm Island," Jonah said, pointing.

"You got a death wish or something?" The policeman didn't bother to remove the whistle from his mouth and it peeped as he spoke. "Can't you see the storm surge is already throwing waves up over the bridge?"

"But I've got to get across!"

"Not on foot, you won't! Anyway the bridge is strictly one way only." He pointed back up the main street. "That way—right out of town!"

The policeman sent Jonah back the way he'd come, but Jonah didn't go far. He halted in a store doorway a little way up the street and watched the police officers for a while as they waved through the traffic. He was still trying to work out a way to slip past them when a big wave threw a plume of spray up over the parapet rails and onto the bridge. An old Buick swerved, skidded, and slid smoothly into the back of the Ford in front. The accident blocked the bridge and the last of the cars that had made it off the island in time ground to a halt. Horns blared. People started shouting and cursing each other.

"That's all we need," Jonah heard the cop say.

The police officers went to sort out the mess and, suddenly, Jonah took the opportunity. He tucked his head down, making himself as small and inconspicuous as possible, and walked straight past them unnoticed. A moment later, he was on the bridge and running.

"Hey, kid! Come back!" Jonah heard a shout and several blasts on a whistle.

Feet thumping, heart pumping, Jonah ran. He splashed through the surge of salt water the waves were constantly throwing up onto the bridge. The waves peeled along lengths of the bridge, tossing arches of spray over his head. Drenched to the skin, he peered through them hoping to see the end, but the stretch of the bridge only seemed to grow longer, arrowing away in front of him, until he began to think he would never reach the far side. He was just over halfway when the first of the big waves hit.

The waves were coming in off the ocean, pushed along by the rising winds, rolling around the point of the island and compacting in the channel behind. Jonah saw the first of them coming and watched it with a practiced eye. It was big—almost as high as the bridge itself—and the concrete shuddered beneath his feet as the wave smacked into the bridge supports and hurled itself over the parapet rails.

It hit with tremendous power and made a crashing sound—like a dozen cannons all firing at once—as it exploded and sent spray flaring into the air. A moment later, it crashed down heavily and the water surged across the bridge. Water swamped the road, spuming and frothing as it drained away between the rails and cascaded back into the sea.

Farther out, Jonah could see bigger waves coming. He ran faster than he had ever run before. He ran through the arches of spray with the salt stinging his face and eyes. He ran until the muscles of his legs felt as if they were on fire and the rasp of his breath made his lungs raw. He was pitting his speed against the waves as they rolled in a deadly race that risked all.

"You're going to make it. You've got to make it!" he gasped, urging himself on. Out of the corner of his eye, he caught tantalizing glimpses of the shore ahead of him. Storm Island was close now. So close. But not close enough.

The next three waves hit one after the other along a fifty-yard stretch on the bridge. They were of awesome size and shook the bridge to its foundation piles with each impact as they rolled in with all the noise and destructive power of a runaway freight train.

Jonah saw them coming and came to a sliding halt. He stared in horrified disbelief as water rose to engulf everything in front of him. It seemed to happen so slowly and yet with terrifying speed. He saw the first wave peel over the parapet rails as it broke right on the bridge. The water curled down the length of the road toward him in slow motion, but accelerated as it approached, until suddenly it was right over his head. He didn't have a chance.

As the water thundered down, it took his legs out from under him and smacked the breath from his body. It enfolded him in its violent, rolling tumble and hurled him across the road. He hit the ground and felt the burning rasp of the concrete as he was pushed mercilessly toward the parapet rails on the other side.

He hit hard but had just enough time to grab the bottom rail, wrapping his arms and legs around it, as the water rushed on past him and over the edge. Holding his head out of the torrent and gasping for breath, he clung there until he felt the stream slacken. Then came the second and third waves.

The weight of the water slammed him flat against the rail. It surged over him and past him. It filled his nose, his mouth, his eyes, and his ears. It knocked the breath out of him and spun him around so that he was hanging over the edge with the sea below. Had he not had his legs wrapped around the rail, the sea would have taken him then. Without mercy. Leaving no trace.

But Jonah's will to live was strong.

He gritted his teeth and held on as the water swamped and battered him, thumping into his body, until inevitably the blows started taking their toll. Each one knocked a little more of the fight out of him. Each one forced him a little closer to letting go. His foot slipped. His legs swung wildly out over the drop and he knew it was only a matter of time before he fell.

Just when he felt he could hold on no longer, the pressure of the water eased. The stream faltered. The solid rush gushed in one final surge then, exhausted, slowed to a trickle.

Free of the relentless pounding, Jonah summoned all his strength and heaved his leg up until he had hooked it over the rail again. He hung there as he recovered a little, then, bit by bit, he hauled himself back up. A moment later, he was flopping out onto the bridge, floundering and gasping on the road like an exhausted fish.

Slowly, painfully, he got to his knees and then to his feet. For a moment, he was disoriented. The constant bursts of spray made it difficult to see and he almost set off in the wrong direction before realizing his mistake. He could see lights ahead and took several faltering steps toward them. The lights seemed to spring out at him. He stopped and was still peering at them when he heard the roar of the engine.

The white pickup burst through the curtains of spray at terrifying speed. Headlights blazing, windshield steamed up, and the wipers sending arcs of water streaming out to either side. It was going flat-out and wasn't going to stop.

"Look out!" Jonah shouted as he hurled himself out of the way at the last moment.

The pickup roared on as Jonah landed and rolled. He looked up and glimpsed the driver's face as he drove by. The man was wide-eyed. Staring. Teeth gritted, lips pulled back in an animal snarl. It was the face of fear.

*

The rain started again. Slow, scattered drops at first, tink-tonking on the metal roofs of the houses. The sky was much darker now, the clouds cut every so often by the silver flicker of lightning.

He rubbed at the ache in his shoulder. His neck felt stiff from being wrenched but apart from that and a few scrapes, he wasn't hurt.

He stood up and glanced back down the hill. Through the rain, he could see the waves swamping the bridge. He had been lucky to make it across at all. He wondered if the driver of the white pickup had been so lucky. He doubted it.

The rain was heavy but warm, and he let it wash the salt from his face. The wind was still rising, savage gusts whirling the fronds of the palms into sudden frenzies and buffeting the traffic lights and road signs.

Storm Island wasn't big, but the houses were spread out along the entire sea front, some hidden among the palms and salt oaks. Sal's address was burned into his brain. Jonah didn't need to look at her letter to see where she lived, but he could see finding his way to Green Turtle Bay wasn't going to be easy. He set off up the hill, looking for someone to ask. Edwin, however, had turned Storm Island into a ghost island.

The houses were boarded up and abandoned. Driveways were emptied of cars. Everywhere he looked, he could see signs that people had moved out in a hurry: the scattered furniture, half-loaded trailers, the clothes left to be blown to rags on the clotheslines, a doll dropped in the middle of the road. But it was only when he crested the hill by a convenience store that he truly understood their hurry.

Without knowing it, he had stumbled to the top of one of the highest points on the island. Ahead, the road glistened, a shining line that dropped down the hill on the other side to curve along the dunes of the seafront. From where he stood, he had an uninterrupted view of the sea for the first time. And, for the first time, he had a chance to look upon Edwin's face.

The size of the storm took his breath away. Towering thunderclouds were heaped up on the horizon like so many exploding skyscrapers. The clouds had swallowed up the sky and turned the sun blood red. The purple-black darkness, like night without the moon or stars, was illuminated only by the lightning as it cut down in sudden slivers of jagged light and cracked the sky, smacking into the water in explosions that stood up like geysers. Edwin was a storm of gargantuan proportions. Brooding. Menacing. Ugly and violent, yet savagely beautiful.

"*Stoirm*," Jonah gasped as he gazed in awe.

Instantly, the storm answered. Lightning flickered, its cold flare reflected on his face. Its brightness cut through his thoughts and he felt the thump of the wind and the sting of the rain once more. Suddenly, he was running again.

Perhaps he just lucked out. Perhaps it was just good fortune that led him to the beach. Or maybe it was something else. Something deeper. Whether drawn there by instinct or not, he knew as soon as he crested the dune and saw the curve of the white sand that he had gone the right way. He knew instantly—it was Sal's place.

He had seen the sign marked Beach (with an arrow, pointing the direction) and had turned off the road, following the wooden walkway that cut through the dips and humps of the dunes almost without thinking.

At first he only had eyes for the sea. The waves were tumultuous, pounding in, curling, spuming plumes of spray yards long from their crests. The houses along the beachfront had been closed up against them, the brightly painted storm shutters bolted across the windows and doors. But as he had stood on the shore with the wind hissing and fizzing, his memory had stirred.

"This is it—I know it is," he told himself, shielding his eyes from the sting of the salt.

The beach curved away beyond a deserted lifeguard's lookout tower to a jumble of rocks on the point where a light shone in the gathering gloom.

The lightning flashed and the lighthouse jumped out of the teeming rain. Squat and solid. A beacon light standing on a slab of rock with the waves crashing at its feet. A single bright point of light shining resolutely against the coming darkness. Remote. Like a star.

The light gave him hope. He ran toward it. The wet sand was firm beneath his feet as he forced himself into the wind. He reached the point, could go no further, and was wondering what to do next when he saw the surfers.

At first, he thought it was his imagination playing tricks on him. The glimpses were brief and only half-seen. They tricked and teased his eyes, forcing him to squint into the wind and rain. But the more he looked, the more he saw.

They were surfing out off the point. Near the beacon light, where the waves were rising and falling over a sandbar. Distant figures sliding across the giant waves. He counted six surfers at least. They seemed so unaware of the danger, he began to believe they weren't people at all. In the froth and boil and tumult of the waves, they seemed more like water spirits or the ghosts of long-dead surfers returned to ride the storm.

As he watched, he saw three break away from the pack and ride the waves in. They hit the beach and, one after the other, came floundering out of the water like exhausted seals.

"Forget it, man!" one of the surfers gasped. "It's suicide on a board out there!"

Only then was Jonah sure they were real. "Wait!" he said, running after them.

He almost lost them in the humps of the dunes, put on a burst of speed, and only just managed to catch up with them in the road beyond.

"What do you want, man?" one yelled, the wind stealing some of his words. "Storm's...going to hit bad!"

Jonah had to shout three times before he managed to make himself heard. "Lost! Is this Green Turtle Bay?" and finally, "Sal—Sally Dayton?"

One of the three pointed and said something he couldn't hear. Jonah looked up the road. By the time he looked back, they had run on. He called after them, but he knew they wouldn't have waited even if they had heard him.

He looked back up the road. The storm made the air seem thick and impenetrable. Here and there among the palms, a streetlight threw down a shaft of light. The lights were dancing crazily in the wind, but beyond them he could just make out a gate and a house set apart from the rest.

He ran toward it, with the light of the lighthouse shining to his right. A wave broke through the dunes and swamped the road. He splashed through the surge as it fell back. Then suddenly he was standing at the gate. There, painted on the side of the metal mailbox on the fence was the name: Dayton.

"Sal!" He called her name over and over again as he ran down the short drive, hurdled the steps onto the verandah and slammed his fists against the storm shutters. "Sal! It's me—Jonah!" he yelled. "Saaaaaaaal!"

But he was too late. Sal had gone.

"Sal!"

Jonah rested his forehead against the storm shutters over the front door. He had hammered on the shutters, shouting her name until his voice was hoarse even though he knew it was useless, and now he was overcome by his disappointment and despair. He fought the tears, but they came all the same, squeezing out of his eyes to trickle through the salt on his cheeks. He sat down, dropping heavily onto the slatted planking of the verandah and leaned against the storm shutters.

"Sal." He said her name without any hope.

The house stood on the edge of the bay within sight of the lighthouse on the point. It fronted onto the beach, less than a hundred yards from the ocean itself. Two stories topped with a tiled roof and walls that jutted at designed angles, surrounded by dunes and palm trees. The house was closed up against him. Wrapped in storm shutters. Locked and bolted. Impregnable.

"She's gone."

The single-minded purpose that had driven him to that place against all the odds left him. All the fight just drained out of him, leaving him to his hopelessness. Listlessly, he sat and watched the rain cascading off the bullnosed roof of the verandah, a beaded-curtain of water that smacked incessantly on the ground just beyond the steps leading up to the front door.

"I should've listened to my dad. I never should have come."

He was still sitting there, head bowed, when lights appeared in the road and a car pulled up in front of the house. Doors opened and thumped shut. Shadows moved across the light and, suddenly, the curtain of rain parted.

Jonah squinted into the glare of the lights, shielding his eyes as he looked up at the girl who just stood staring back at him with the rain running in rivulets off her yellow waterproof jacket, soaking her cutoffs and dripping down her bare legs. She was soaked to the skin and her hair hung in dark rat's tails around her face, but she was smiling.

"Sal," Jonah whispered.

She glanced over her shoulder. "Dan! Connie!" she called. "You'd better come quick!"

*

Meeting his long-lost sister for the first time wasn't at all like Jonah had imagined it would be. No big hugs. No tears. Just an awkward silence as they stood dripping in a hallway, looking at each other with the storm cracking and flashing outside.

"I don't understand," Dan said, rubbing at the steam on the lenses of his round, wire-rimmed glasses. "Are you a friend of Sal's?"

Jonah shook his head.

"Then who are you?"

"My name's Jonah—Jonah Ebbers. I'm Sal's—"

"Brother," Sal finished for him.

Dan and Connie looked at him as if he were King Zog from the planet Zargoob.

"It's impossible!" Dan said, recovering a little. "We would know if she had a brother...."

Connie, meanwhile, was looking at Jonah intently. She tucked a wayward strand of hair back behind one ear and studied his face. Jonah returned her gaze steadily.

"Take a look, Dan," she said quietly.

After a moment's hesitation, Dan frowned, stepped forward, and squinted at Jonah. He opened his mouth as if he was about to say something, thought better of it, and closed it again.

Sal reached out and touched Jonah's face. She smiled. "I knew you'd come."

"Will you stop saying that!" Dan said. He glared at Jonah. "Can you prove you're who you say you are?"

"Dan!" Connie hissed. "Stop shouting and give the kid a chance. He's only wearing board shorts and a T-shirt. Where's he supposed to keep I.D.?"

"But how do we know he's telling the truth?" Dan said. "He could be anyone! Maybe he was looting. Maybe he saw us leave. Maybe he thought it was safe to break into the place. Maybe he didn't know the bridge had been blocked and we couldn't get off the island!"

"I didn't want to leave," Sal said. She ignored Dan and spoke to Jonah. "Dan made me."

"I sure did, my girl!" Dan interrupted. "And look where locking yourself in your room has got us—stuck here with no place to go. It'd be too dangerous to leave now even if we could. We're just going to have to stay here and sweat it out, so you had better hope the house is strong enough to take the pounding." He looked at Jonah again. "And if I'm going to share my place with you, then I have a right to know who you are."

"I'm Jonah—Sal's brother."

Dan threw up his hands. "That's it! I've had enough of this."

Jonah remembered the letter. He dug into the pocket of his shorts and pulled it out. The paper was soaked and the letter tore. It came out in pieces, a mess of smudged ink.

Sal reached out and took what remained of the letter, glanced at it, then handed it to Connie.

The disbelief sighed out of Connie and she deflated onto a chair. "Sal was right."

"Let me see that letter." Dan took it and what was left of it disintegrated in his hands. "This doesn't prove a thing!"

Connie looked up at Dan. "She sent that letter about a month ago. I didn't tell you because I knew what you would say." She sighed. "I thought it was better to let her send it. She had written before. Three, maybe four, times. She'd never gotten a reply."

"That's because the letters got lost," Jonah said, but he didn't explain how or why. "And I was going to write, but then Dad said we were coming to see Sal and there didn't seem any point."

"He's here?" Sal said, startled. She hadn't considered that her father might have come, too.

Jonah nodded. "We got split up in Bridgewater because of the storm. The police were evacuating everyone. He wanted me to get on the bus. I should've stayed with him, but I had to find you. I had to warn you about Edwin."

Dan snorted. "Warn us about the storm! That's lame! It's only been reported on every radio and TV station. Didn't you think we'd heard?"

"You don't understand. It's more than that. It was the Bone Man." Jonah tried to explain but he could tell by the look on Dan's face that he was only making things worse. "Look I know you don't believe me, but I think something bad is going to happen, something very bad if we don't get away from here."

"Too late," Dan said. "The bridge is closed." He began pacing up and down, then stopped and looked at Jonah. "Why didn't you call? Don't they have phones in Ireland?"

"We tried but we didn't get an answer," Jonah said. "It isn't easy phoning international from the pay phone in The Crooked Finger. And anyway it all happened so fast. Dad sold his motorcycle and bought the tickets and suddenly we were here. Then the storm hit."

"We've been away," Connie admitted.

"Don't say you believe him!" Dan groaned. "He could have found that letter, picked it up—anything." He rolled his eyes. "And haven't we been through this a thousand times? The adoption agency would have told us if she had a brother."

"But my dad didn't tell them about me," Jonah started to explain, but the wind interrupted, thumping against the front of the house. There was a loud crash as something fell.

No one spoke for a while.

Then Connie broke the silence. "He's telling the truth, Dan," she said. "You just have to look at his face to see that."

Dan ran his hand through his hair and shook his head, sending drips flying. "I still say it's impossible."

"How can it be if he's here, Dan?" Connie said. "He's come, just like Sal said." She gave Jonah a look as if she couldn't really believe it herself. "Sal said the storm would bring you. That's why she didn't want to leave. She was afraid you would come when she wasn't here and she would never know. She even locked herself in her room. That's why we didn't get away before they closed the bridge to the mainland."

Connie turned to Sal and took her gently by the shoulders. "And I said you were wrong. I told you it was impossible and that it was all in your head, like the dreams and the other things you've had over the years."

"I always knew," Sal said. She looked at Jonah. "It was like part of me was missing."

Connie looked at Dan. "That was the reason I encouraged her to write to her father in Ireland," she said. "I thought it would help her come to terms with the past. I thought it would prove once and for all she was wrong about her make-believe brother."

She turned to Jonah. "Somehow Sal has always known about you. I don't know how, but for as long as she has been able to talk, she's been telling us about her brother who lives across the sea." She sighed and shook her head. "We never believed her."

As Connie spoke, the last piece of a puzzle fell into place for Jonah and he saw the whole picture for the first time. He and Sal were linked. Invisibly. Intangibly. Inextricably. They were like two halves of a whole. Different and yet one.

A shutter broke loose somewhere and started banging. Dan hurried away to close it, and when he came back, his face was grim.

"The sea is up over the dunes," he said. "It's not safe to stay down here. We'd better get upstairs. Now! Before the house floods."

As he spoke, the lights flickered, brightened momentarily again, then died.

*

Darkness came at midday. Like an eclipse, the daylight faded and a shadow fell over Storm Island as Hurricane Edwin finally hit. With wind speeds of more than 150 miles an hour, it seemed to scoop up the ocean and hurl it at the shore. The waves rose up over the dunes and raced up around the houses along the beach front, swamping the gardens, driveways, and roads.

The lightning became a constant flicker, a black-and-white movie of light and dark that illuminated the palm trees as they bowed before the storm. But their supplications were not enough. In twos and threes, the storm dispatched them without mercy. Tearing them up by the roots and hurling them away with violence and noise.

"Houses like these are designed to survive most storms," Dan said. But they all knew that Hurricane Edwin was no ordinary storm.

Edwin mashed and stirred the dark cauldron of the waters and drove the waves against the shore, sending towers of glintless spray high into the air. The lightning bolts dropped. The thunder cracked and rolled. It was as if the world had become encased inside a huge machine—a machine of awesome proportions—and was being driven to destruction by some crazed Captain Nemo.

They could only sit and await their fate, talking about small discomforts in a futile attempt to forget the large.

"You would have thought it would get cooler with the rain," Connie observed, "but it doesn't. It just gets hotter."

"Latent heat." Dan said and added, "The eye of the storm must be getting close now."

Dan had found two flashlights. They used one, keeping one in reserve, just in case. They had taken off their waterproof jackets, dried off with towels, and were sitting on the floor of the bedroom at the back of the house. It was the farthest away from the sea and, Dan said, was the safest if the house flooded.

Gradually, they fell silent and listened to the storm. Jonah watched as Sal fingered her necklaces. She was wearing at least half a dozen, some silver, others leather and beaded. One in particular caught his eye.

"Shark's tooth," she said, when she noticed him looking at it.

She held it so it dangled on its thong and caught the light. The tooth was wedge-shaped and almost as long as Jonah's little finger. She smiled. "The surfie who sold it to me said it was lucky. It's supposed to keep the sharks away. But it doesn't work. Tiger Shark took a fancy to my board while I was surfing in Green Turtle Bay about a month ago."

Jonah sat up sharply and looked at her. "A month! But that's exactly when—"

"Can we talk about something else!" Connie interrupted. "I don't like hearing about that shark."

"But—" Jonah tried again.

Dan cut him off. "I want everyone thinking positive thoughts right now."

That was easier said than done with the wind throwing itself ceaselessly at the house. The gusts hit with such force that the whole building shook. Every now and then, something fell with a thump. The noises became a percussion of small things breaking, an accompaniment to the great symphony the wind played on the wires and in the hollows outside.

All the while the Unblinking Eye moved closer.

The house rocked, shuddering to its foundations. The rain smacked on the roof like pebbles. The wind levered away the tiles and sent them spinning away to shatter and smash. The house was breaking up around them. Little by little. Piece by piece.

Edwin pummeled the house, sending mighty waves to scoop away the dunes so the full weight of water could be brought to bear on the walls.

Slowly, inexorably, the sea began to undermine the front of the house.

"Tell me about Ireland," Sal said, when their silence became oppressive.

"What do you want to know?"

Sal shrugged. "Anything. Everything."

So Jonah told her about Mulligan. At first, he found it difficult. He had lived there all his life and it seemed too familiar to be interesting, but Sal insisted. As he spoke, he was surprised how easy it became.

He told her about White Bird Cottage and how their mother had named it. He described the harbor and the boats, and told her about Fergus and the thrill of finding a good lobster in the pot when he pulled it up from the sea bed. He spoke of the mist and the way the dolphins always came back to the bay. He even told her about Megan. Then, finally, he told her about Skullcrack, about the waves and the way the sea spread wide below Craxkull Point.

Sal listened intently until he finished, then, without a word, she stood up and picked up the spare flashlight.

"Where are you going?" Dan asked.

"I have to show Jonah something in my room."

Sal's room was the second on the right at the front of the house. She handed him the flashlight and he played the beam across the posters and onto the surfboard that stood in the corner by the window. He could see part of the tail had been bitten away. Sal asked him to point the flashlight at her desk and she slid open the drawer, rummaging through the papers until she pulled out a paper with a pencil sketch on it.

Jonah shined the flashlight on the picture and there, in the circle of light, was Craxkull Point. The black rocks in the mist. The cliff towering away into a sky where white birds stood out against gray clouds.

"You see," Sal said. "I've always known."

Jonah was still looking at the picture in amazement when the storm came and took them.

*

Edwin's hand came suddenly, punching out of the darkness to scoop away the front of the house. The foundations of the wall, which had been undermined and weakened by the constant battering, gave way under the strain and sent cracks racing up the walls. The house groaned as if mortally wounded. Edwin tore at it, ripping it apart as if it were a doll's house.

Sal's warning shout was lost in Edwin's roar as the floor sagged. The desk, bed, surfboard— everything—slid away from them. Jonah dropped the flashlight as he slipped and fell, scrambling for a hold on the floor that was suddenly tilting as if it were the deck of a sinking ship.

He heard Sal's scream as she slid down the slope, her legs kicking helplessly as she disappeared into the dark water. Then he, too, felt the splintered sharpness of the edge and fell with an awesome rush.

Jonah hit the water and went under. He came up and was immediately dragged out as the waves receded. Another wave thundered in, collecting him like a piece of flotsam and pushing him back toward the house.

The front of the house rushed toward him. The front wall had collapsed and all the rooms inside were open to the elements. The water rushed in downstairs, the surge thrusting him into the gaping maw of what had once been the front room. Like the mouth of a giant whale, the house sucked Jonah in and drank him down in a jumble of floating furniture. He had just enough time to brace his legs before he slammed into the wall at the far end of the room, then the weight of water rammed him into a doorway that opened like a monstrous gullet before him. He became wedged among the debris and furniture.

Desperately, Jonah fought to break free of the tangled wreckage. He fought, straining with all his strength, but no sooner had he freed himself than the waves crushed him into the narrow gap again. His head slipped through, but his shoulders wedged. Jagged, searing pain tore through him, pushing an agonized groan from his lips. He summoned all his strength and pushed back, managing to pull his head out of the water.

Then, as quickly as it had surged in, the water drew back, sucking up everything that moved with it. Jonah saw a flashlight beam through the rain. He saw Dan's face and Connie's too, lit up by lightning. Their mouths were open but their shouts were lost on the tumult. He saw an outstretched hand and grabbed for it. It was Sal. She was clinging to a piece of wreckage. Their fingers met and clasped.

"Hold on!" she was shouting.

The house receded and a weighty darkness engulfed them as they were dragged out into the churning waters of the bay.

The fierce riptide pulled Jonah and Sal out swiftly. Helpless, they could only cling to the wreckage that went with them until a wave reared up and smashed it from Jonah's grasp. He was immediately swamped and went under. Once. Twice. Each time driven down farther.

It was a strange feeling. Below the waves he found only great calmness. A gentle quiet. An endless soothing swish of the warm water. There, the storm that raged over his head was unable to touch him.

Stay here, Jo! a voice whispered. *You're safe here. Why fight it? Why go back to the storm?*

The voice tempted and persuaded him with promises of endless peace and Jonah let it soothe him as he began to drift between the layers of dark water. He would have stayed there, had the mermaid with Sal's face not found him.

She came down from above, swimming fast, flitting through the darkness to catch him by his T-shirt. He felt her pulling him up, and as he rose toward the surface, he became aware of the terrible burning in his lungs. The pain cut through the dark mist that threatened to overwhelm him and, suddenly, he was fighting to reach the air.

They shot up out of the water together, gasping, as they clung to each other. A brief moment of panic, then Sal managed to catch hold of something floating nearby. It was a big piece of her surfboard—the tail section, with the chunk chewed out. The leash was still attached. She strapped it around Jonah's wrist so the waves couldn't pluck it from him while he coughed the water from his lungs. Together they clung to the board and let it carry them.

"Don't you...go drowning...on me...now, little brother!" Sal shouted, above the noise.

"You should have left me," Jonah gasped back. "The storm wants me. I know it does."

"Don't be stupid! Shut up and hold on!"

And that's what they did, for what seemed like an eternity, too exhausted to do anything else.

*

The brightness, when it came, was so startling that at first Jonah thought he must have drowned without even realizing it. The wind dropped suddenly, racing away to howl in the distance. He felt a warm breeze, a breeze so gentle it might have been stirred by the soft beat of a wing.

He lifted his head and stared into the Unblinking Eye itself. Only then did he see Edwin's true majesty.

In the eye of the storm, all was peaceful. The sky had telescoped away to a circle of blue high above. All around it, the clouds towered in a cylindrical wall. Shades of gray. Heaped up high. Encircling them within their monumental power. The wind in the distance, howling like a million furious demons that had been shut out.

Within this citadel of cloud, however, the ranks of waves that had marched so determinedly toward the shore were left suddenly leaderless.

Confused, they lost direction. It seemed the will of the Unblinking Eye had wavered in its terrible purpose and now gazed benignly upon them. Watching. Weighing their lives in the balance as if the great god of destruction was deciding whether to take pity on them.

It was their chance.

"The light!" Sal shook Jonah and pointed.

He saw the beacon shining like a bright star against the darkness. The lighthouse standing resolutely on the point. Tiny compared to the storm that surrounded it, but close. Very close.

"We can make it!" Sal shook him to action. "Swim, Jonah! Swim!"

Jonah nodded, too exhausted to speak. He was feeling strangely light-headed and was afraid he might pass out. Everything was suddenly strange, warm and quiet and slow, and he began to think it was all just a dream. A dream in which he could be awake and asleep at the same time.

They kicked toward the rocks, rising high over the crests of the waves and sinking deep into the troughs, until they reached the shore. A wave lifted them over the rocks. They caught hold. The water receded a moment later, leaving them stranded and gulping for breath.

"We can't stay here!" Sal urged him on. "The Eye is passing. We have to get to the tower."

Once again, the dizziness almost overwhelmed Jonah as he struggled to his feet. Exhausted as he was, he still recognized a stirring in the wind as Sal helped him to his feet. The dream world was suddenly threatened by the return of nightmares, and the terror of what would come drove him on. Weary beyond all weariness, he stumbled toward the lighthouse tower. The board was still attached to his wrist and it bobbed over the rocks as he dragged it along.

A few scrubby bushes grew around the base of the tower where a metal door had been fixed into the stone on the leeward side. A sign warned them: KEEP OUT! MAINTENANCE PERSONNEL ONLY. When Sal tried the rusted handle, it wouldn't budge.

"It has to!" Jonah's desperation gave him strength. He leaned on the handle with all his weight and felt it shift. He pushed down again and again. He was working so intently on what he was doing, Sal had to push him aside to make him stop.

"It's open!"

Jonah blinked at the handle stupidly. Sal pulled at the open door. The hinges creaked and sent tiny pieces of rust jumping. Inside, several stone steps spiraled up the curving wall toward the light. It was cramped and dark, but there was space enough for two.

They helped each other in, Jonah still dragging the useless piece of board after him on its leash, then pulled the door closed behind them. The darkness was instant and complete. The sheer blackness swamped them.

Jonah leaned heavily against the wall. A wave of dizziness swept over him. His knees buckled and he collapsed onto the cold stone of the floor.

And there, the demons found him.

As the eye of the storm moved on, the wind roared back, and with it came the demons. Like a barbarian horde, they came in a shrieking attack. On lightning steeds they rode the wind, racing across the water to hurl their fury against the lighthouse.

It was as if by some secret arrangement all the demons of his life had gathered to carry him off. They came from far away, quitting their lightless holes in White Bird Cottage and casting off their shadowy cloaks to reveal the true scale of their loathsomeness. With bent bodies and pig-beast faces, they hurled themselves at the tower, whirling and dancing, jabbing and clawing at the stone with their crooked fingers as they dashed themselves to pulp against the stone.

Heeeeeeee'sssss ouuuursss! Give him back! Ou-uuuuuurssssssssssssssssssssss! they hissed and snarled, outraged by Jonah's escape.

Again and again, they threw themselves at the tower, until finally they gathered for one last massive attack. Riding on the crest of a giant wave, they broke against the stone with force enough to crack it and put out the beacon light. For one terrifying moment, the tower seemed sure to fall. It groaned and shuddered. The door burst open and seawater poured in.

Sal grappled with the door. Jonah grabbed hold of the handle. Together, they pushed. The door began to close. They heaved as one. Their combined effort narrowed the gap little by little, while the demons marshaled all their forces to bend and wrench at it.

Alone, Jonah would never have managed. It took every bit of his strength and Sal's to close that door. Outside, the demons howled in fury. He could see them spitting lightning snakes. He heard their demented shrieks, echoing endlessly like the raucous cries of a million gulls.

*

When Jonah opened his eyes, he found himself lying with his cheek pressed against the cold stone. He heard a shriek and sat up quickly. He recognized the cries as those of a seagull and breathed a sigh of relief.

Stiff and blinking in the pale light, he looked around. The door of the tower was open. The remains of Sal's surfboard lay beside him, still attached to his wrist. Sal was gone.

"Sal!" he croaked and tried to get up. His legs gave way beneath him and he was forced to crawl to the door. "Sal! Where are you!"

Through the open door he could see the waves breaking around them, only now they were ponderous and heavy in the pink dawn light.

He pulled himself to his feet and leaned heavily on the door frame. After a moment's rest, he staggered out and looked around. He was alone. The sky had lifted and the clouds racing overhead exaggerated the very stillness of the lighthouse.

The light had been smashed from the top and a black crack ran from the top down to its base. All over the rounded stone walls, there were deep scratches scored into the stone, as if the tower had been clawed. He reached out, and as he touched one, a shiver of dread ran through him.

"The waves throw up rocks. They do that," Sal said suddenly.

Jonah spun around at the sound of her voice.

"Sal! Where were you? I looked. I thought—" His lips cracked as he worked them into words and he tasted his own blood. He glanced back at the scratches. "I thought they had—" He paused again, then shook his head. "Forget it."

"I've been as far along the point as I could go," she said. "The waves are breaking right over the rocks so we can't get back that way."

Jonah looked out over Green Turtle Bay, surveying the damage Hurricane Edwin had wrought on shore. Among the fallen trees, he could see the ruins of the houses. The destruction was complete. He knew Sal was thinking about Connie and Dan.

"Do you think...."

She didn't answer. "I reckon we'll just have to swim," she said.

That was all she said.

Jonah turned the bone in his fingers so it caught the sunlight. It was almost time to leave. Coot had warned them not to be too long or they'd miss the bus back to Orlando.

Almost a week had passed since Jonah and Sal had paddled in together on the remains of Sal's board and washed up on the shore. There, Connie and Dan had found them, and later, at what was left of the house, his father.

"Jo!" his father had been sobbing as he had enveloped him in a bear hug. He had been too relieved to be angry. "I looked everywhere. I couldn't find you."

Jonah glanced up at the dunes where his father and Sal sat side by side. They still looked awkward together, their movements stiff and uncomfortable as they talked softly.

He decided Mr. Morran had been right about one thing at least, the past did touch the present. He knew it would affect their future, too. Finding Sal had only been the beginning. She had her own life with Connie and Dan, and he wondered whether there truly was room for them all in it. He made up his mind to give her the book of poetry and the photograph of her with their mother. He knew they would help.

He fisted the bone and stood up, startling a gull off the wet sand as he walked down to the water's edge. The gull lifted effortlessly to hang above him on the breeze. The water ran up around his feet gurgling softly as he looked out at the surfers riding the waves near the wrecked lighthouse.

He glanced down at the bone, weighing it in his hand. After a moment's thought, he pulled his arm back and sent it spinning away. It made no splash as it hit the water.

"*Slán agat, Edwin,*" he said, and with that goodbye, he looked east. Out there somewhere lay Ireland and Skullcrack, waiting for him.

He watched a magnificent wave bump up, and he rode it in his mind. Feet planted firmly on his board, he was electric. Unstoppable. The exhilaration burst out of him in a shout as the lip curled, dropping to touch the trough and forming a tube pierced by sparkles of light. He crouched low on his board and hurtled down the silvery-blue pipe as it flexed and curved like steel.

In that frozen moment, time ceased to have meaning. He was aware only of the ocean. It seemed to flow through him as if he was part of its vastness, its greatness, and in the surf's thunderous roar, he heard Edwin's last, defiant shout.

High above, the white bird lost interest and turned away on the wind.

*

Megan sat on the cliff of Craxkull Point and watched the white bird as it lifted high over her head. It hung in the air, legs tucked back, watching her as it soared on the breeze.

She looked down at the postcard she held tightly in her hand: Greetings from Cape Canaveral. A picture of a rocket climbing, engines flaring against the blue of the Florida sky, trailing a plume of smoke that billowed out behind like a huge, puffed flower.

She smiled.

"From that boyfriend of yours, isn't it," Billy asked.

She sighed and looked up to find her brother watching her from a safe distance. "He's not my boyfriend."

"Is so," Billy insisted. "I read it."

"Well, you had no right!"

Billy grinned. "And he must be your boyfriend because he says he loves you."

"He does not say that!"

"Does too! Right there on the bottom after the bit about coming home soon. There! See! 'Love from Jonah.' "

Megan rolled her eyes as Billy made stupid wooing noises at her. She shook her head. "How can you be my brother, Billy Doherty?"

"It isn't easy," Billy admitted, deciding it was safe enough to sit down. He kicked his feet over the drop, until Megan made him come back.

There was a long pause before Billy spoke:

"I don't believe all that stuff about how he found his sister in the middle of that hurricane," he said as if he had given it a lot of careful consideration. "It's just a load of rubbish."

"Oh yes, and what do you know about twins?"

"Loads," Billy said modestly.

Megan gave up and gazed out at the sea spread wide and green below Craxkull Point. The sun dropped a shaft of bright light that caught a wave. She noticed the way the light sparkled on the curl of the lip as it thundered over Skullcrack. She watched it roll in, majestic and beautiful, standing proud for a moment before it fell in a breathtaking burst of white on the black rocks of Craxkull Point.

Billy shook his head. "Nah, I don't believe in none of that weird stuff," he said, looking out at the waves.

But unlike his sister, who had always been able to see far beyond what was plainly obvious, he saw only sky and sea.

Dance there upon the shore;
What need have you to care
For wind or water's roar?
W. B. Yeats

The word "twins" is derived from the ancient German word "twin" or "twine," which means "two together." Scientists have discovered that twins are linked together in some fascinating ways. Twins who have been reared apart often claim to experience a powerful bond with their missing co-twin, sometimes even sharing the pain of a sister or brother whom they have never met. When they do finally meet, they often discover that they share some eerie similarities in personality and behavior.

One famous case of reunited twins is that of Jerry Levey and Mark Newman of New Jersey. When a friend of Newman's reunited the two, Newman was shocked to encounter a carbon copy of himself—one who had, by chance, been living only 65 miles away from him. Their life stories were remarkably similar: each was a volunteer firefighter; each had planned to study the same subject in college; both loved John Wayne movies and fishing. Both would drink only one kind of beer, and they even held the can in the same way, with the pinkie finger curled underneath. After their reunion, each reported feeling that a gap had been filled in his life. "I used to feel something was missing," said Newman. "Now it's back in place."

Many other twins have experienced a powerful yearning to be reunited. Adam and Ida Paluch were separated during World War II when the Nazis raided the Polish ghetto of Sosnowiec, forcing their mother to abandon them. As a child,

Adam ran away each year as soon as the snow began to fall in hopes of finding his family. Ida telephoned all over the world in search of Adam. By the time they found each other, their struggle to reunite their family had lasted 52 years.

Medical science has long documented the fact that some twins experience a connection with their missing counterpart. Doctor Louis Keith of Northwestern University Medical School reports hearing of multiple incidences of shared pain between twins. In one case, a woman felt a searing pain when her twin sister's plane crashed in the Canary Islands; in another, a girl was physically aware of her sister's appendectomy.

The sense of togetherness felt by many twins makes them valuable for scientific research, for genetics in particular. Scientists study twins who were reared apart to better understand how much of our physical and mental makeup is inherited and how much is shaped by our environment. But because of more enlightened practices on the part of adoption agencies, the percentage of twins who grow up in separate households has dwindled to near zero and continues to decrease.

On the other hand, twinning rates are skyrocketing, making the need for twin studies all the more urgent. Worldwide, there are more than 125 million living people who were the products of multiple births. In the United States alone, there are 50,375 sets of twins born each year— 2.6 percent of all births. In the United States, a pregnant woman's chances of giving birth to twins are roughly one in 38.